HAIL
LINSENBIGLER!

BRIAN M. WIPRUD

DEDICATION

For Joanne, as ever and always.

ACKNOWLEDGMENTS

Many thanks to my editors, who like Linsenbigler, would prefer to remain out of the limelight. Special thanks to Skip Baker for his yeoman's work on the cover.

CHAPTER 1

I WAS THRUST INTO HYSTERICAL CONDEMNATION after I was recorded dynamite fishing in Russia.

Prior to my fall from grace, I enjoyed the adulation of our nation as an All-American hero. Not that I deserved the accolades. By my own estimation, I am a borderline drunkard and modest traveling fly angler who was fashioned whole-cloth into a hero by my employer, Conglomerated Beverages. The fact that I have twice found myself in dire circumstance (as a result of my renown) and managed to save my skin is purely the result of a robust desire to survive until the next cocktail hour. By my publicist's twisty logic, and the media's perverse intent, these 'adventures' made me a hero. I was even being eyed by politicians as an electoral thoroughbred.

Alas, there is only one thing the media and the populace embrace more fervently than a hero.

An antihero.

A fallen angel.

A disgraced celebrity.

My assertion that the hand grenade fishing was coerced by Vladimir Putin made my protestations sound ridiculous. Though my assertion was true, I had no evidence to back up my 'wild claim.' There were dark corners of the internet where my pedigree as a hero were already grist for the blogosphere mill. From these outliers came cries of "Ah ha!" Their suspicions of Linsenbigler as a liar and a rank phony were confirmed and ripe for viral acceptance.

In short order, Boone Linsenbigler, dashing pitchman for Conglomerated Beverages' full line of Boone Linsenbigler cocktail amenities, was a pariah.

My publicist Terry Orbach nearly had an aneurism over this calamity – in spite of his epic attempts to prop me up. Poor Terry: an Icarus to my Daedalus. He'd come by my apartment literally weeping with dismay, his long rubbery proboscis dripping with mucus (I have oft before compared poor Terry to a human-sized weevil.) He had been sacked – fired for allowing my brand's ship to founder on the rocks of scandal. Alas, the captain was doomed along with his ship. But Terry's sorrow transformed into defiance – he vowed to right this great wrong and reinstate my good name and his position at Conglomerated. Boone Linsenbigler would once again be the paragon of American heroism and trademarked cocktailing products!

My skepticism of Terry's optimistic decrees were summarily rewarded the following day when I was summoned before the grey-haired men in suits at Conglomerated's skyscraper boardroom. Wood paneled walls bracketed a long narrow table, each side lined with stern faces, a gauntlet of corporate calculus.

At the far end of the table stood an angular man in a three-piece suit whose slicked black hair had grey racing stripes down the sides. This was the CEO of Conglomerated Beverages, none other than Prentis Hargreaves, and he looked every bit of his name. His steel blue eyes surveyed me with thinly disguised pity, and a grin flickered on his tight lips. He seemed the type that enjoyed firing people while pretending he didn't.

My brand, he informed me, had 'cycled out.' Yet he shared a moment of silence and glances with his compatriots before he cleared his throat, arched an eyebrow at me and said: "However…"

The Linsenbigler brand's death sentence had been commuted. My contract had been sold to an African beverage manufacturer: Amalgamated Consumables.

Apparently, market studies indicated that Africans generally thought the hand grenade fishing was amusing, not an atrocity. As such, my brand still had value, but only in the southern hemisphere of our planet where deploying munitions in the act of pescaticide is not a moral crime.

I took the news and my contract to my lawyer for confirmation that this was indeed my only option under the circumstances. Could I really be sold like so much chattel to Amalgamated?

My lawyer, Bubby Hecklin, was a stout man with all the charm of a constipated undertaker. He flipped angrily through my contract, all the while muttering profanities. His dismay over my original contract language with Conglomerated – which had not been vetted by any lawyer prior to signing – was once again in evidence. After a guttural moan, he slapped the contract onto the desk and squinted his dark eyes at mine: "You're fucked, Linsenbigler."

I'm a pretty good writer, a better drinksologist, and an even better angler. Clearly, I am inept when it comes to tending to legal matters. Conglomerated dangled the money; I signed the contract without understanding it.

As per the language of the original five-year 'transferable' contract, I was obliged to meet my pitchman's commitments for the entire term or forfeit all of my earnings. Of course, I no longer had the money to return to them. I had spent a large portion of it. To default on the contract meant bankruptcy and a return to my former life as a freelance writer drinking plastic-bottle vodka in a Jersey basement apartment.

My previous fishing trips to the tropics and Russia had each turned into the most horrendous and blood-curdling calamities, so I was set against subjecting myself to yet another trip to parts unknown.

However, were I to steel myself for two years plus in Africa, I could find myself free and clear of multinational beverage companies once I completed my contractual obligations. My stipends were such that I could likely save enough to go on permanent vacation. Not lavishly, mind you, but there would be enough to set myself up and sustain myself with royalties from my bitters. Location? Somewhere in the tropics with a modest beachside home, dock and fishing skiff. Once I sold my Brooklyn penthouse, I could support myself in a manner to which I could *become* accustomed. As a happy has-been.

Has-been? I admit that rankled my pride just a little.

I never much liked the fame anyway; it made me feel like an imposter.

With the heavy heart of a man doomed to exile, I slogged to my Brooklyn penthouse, the large windows lit only by streetlamp gloom twenty stories below. I shed my overcoat, which was slicked with sleet. Kicking off my wet shoes, I shivered and made tracks for my rattan bar. It was a forlorn night that demanded a dram of peaty Islay single-malt scotch.

This scene was eerily similar to New Year's Eve. On that occasion, I had returned to my dark penthouse in a panic over my soaring, meteoric fame. Three months later, there I was returning to the dark penthouse in a panic over my Hindenburg crash of fame. Damned ironic. Much had changed in a few short months.

Scotch in hand, I fired up my laptop as I had on New Year's Eve. Yet instead of checking my email (which was devoid of any good cheer – my 'friends' had vanished) I typed in the name of the country in which Amalgamated's headquarters were situated: *Zarenga Chi.*

My knowledge of African geography was shaky at

best. I imagined a vast savannah teeming with lions, zebras and giraffes, swaddled tribespeople moving to and fro with jugs of water on their heads. Yet to my surprise, Zarenga Chi was an archipelago located in the Indian Ocean just off the coast of the African continent. *What in blazes would a large company like Amalgamated be doing situated in a backwater like that?*

Scrolling down, I found that Zarenga Chi's economy was rated as the most liberal on the planet. Corporations could locate headquarters there and pay little or no taxes. Zarenga Chi was also a haven for offshore banking. All this at the behest and favor of his Royal Highness – 'Chi' apparently means 'Kingdom' in Zarengi.

That got me laughing. Look around – how much more of a circus could a kingdom be than a democracy?

I sipped scotch with more vigor as I flipped through photos of palm trees, beaches, blue waters, sleek corporate headquarters, sprawling gated communities and – what have we here? – leaping fish!

By all appearances, Zarenga Chi was a sport fishing paradise for everything from wahoo and sailfish to giant trevally and bonefish. The only reason I had not heard of it was because the place had no fishing lodges open to the public. Ordinary slobs and riffraff need not apply. The country was in effect one giant gated community, a resort nation catering to banking and corporate elite. This was *their* playground – exclusively.

Now it would be *my* playground.

In the Bahamas and Mexico, I had been forced to

tangle with smugglers and drug lords. In Russia, I had fallen prey to the whims of international espionage. Zarenga Chi, however, was like a corporate citadel, a veritable fortress clad against the world's base evils.

Ice rattled in my glass as my anxiety was replaced with growing exultation.

To hell with dreary Brooklyn's never-ending parade of slush! To hell with the scornful public! And to hell with Prentis Hargreaves!

Hail, Zarenga Chi – I am yours!

CHAPTER 2

MOVING TO AFRICA for two years is not like going on a vacation.

First, I had to figure out what to do with my current dwelling – you can't just turn off the lights and close the door. Options included subletting it, but after considerable deliberation I decided to engage the services of a real estate agent and sell it lock, stock and bar. The market was strong in Brooklyn, and as I did not know what my situation would be two years hence, much less the real estate scene, it seemed wise to cash out and keep that money in reserve for the tropical bungalow of which I'd dreamt.

Secondly, you cannot obtain a two and a half year visa or work permit to Zarenga Chi. The legions of foreign nationals who call it home must apply for citizenship. The U.S. has no problem with dual citizenship per se except inasmuch as they have little power to broker your safe return from the clutches of a foreign judicial system.

Amalgamated Consumables arranged an emissary from Zarenga's New York embassy to guide me through the process, and I felt like a new hire indoctrinated by a corporate human resources department. Somewhat ominously, it wasn't until April Fools' Day that I was summoned to collect my passport. Just as well it took as long as it did as it afforded me time to dispatch my penthouse in the meantime. I priced it to sell quickly.

Oddly, nobody from Amalgamated had yet approached with what was expected of me once I was in their midst. I was already effectively their employee, and yet I had not been tasked with any photo or commercial shoots. One would have thought that my proximity to numerous production studios would have inspired some principal photography as the Cocktail King of Africa. I presumed something must be going on behind the scenes and that I should gird myself for a promotional juggernaut once they had me in their grasp.

While I spent my last two weeks in New York lodged at a midtown hotel – nothing fancy, mind you – I was conscious of saving my resources for two plus years down the line. And I wanted to feel free to indulge in some of the fine bars and taverns Manhattan had to offer.

When I returned from my last exploit, the one in Russia, necessity had dictated that I cut my hair and mustache short. The effect was fortunate – I was not immediately recognizable as the famous Boone Linsenbigler with the magnificent whiskers and jaunty locks of hair. As a pariah, it was best to maintain this appearance so as not to be castigated at every corner bar. So my hair was close-cropped and parted, my mustache pencil-thin. I had decided that if asked I would say my name was Felix, though any bartender that inspected my credit card was sure to know who I was and sneer at will.

The first week, I spent my days at the gym and at libraries and book stores reading up on Africa and Zarenga Chi in particular. Oh, yes, and researching the type of fishing tackle I would need for saltwater big game fly fishing. My room at the hotel soon came to resemble a tackle shop. Evenings were spent making the rounds of the posh midtown bars like King Cole, Sir Harry's, 21 Club and Bemelmans. Drinks are all over twenty dollars each. The vibe in these places make you feel stupendously rarified, and the nuts are free. One actually served free quail eggs. So I was putting on the Ritz before my banishment.

While I am fully capable of rigging my own sloop and sailing alone, there were pangs of loneliness for a first mate. I had tried to track down Tanya, a DEA agent I had spent some time with in Nassau. I knew she wouldn't cut me lose over the grenade fishing incident and thought maybe I could fly her to New York for the weekend. Alas, she had left teaching at Quantico and was "on assignment," which I assumed meant that she had resumed undercover work. This surprised me because she claimed to have lost her nerve after being tortured in the Bahamas.

On Saturday morning my ship literally came in.

It was the Queen Mary.

The ship's dance instructor Miranda texted me that they had docked and that she would be in New York for the week. She was shapely and spirited, and we had had a liaison aboard the Queen Mary when I sailed to London four months back. What a pleasant surprise, as I did not even recall giving her my phone number.

Clapping my hands together and giving them a good rub, I began to plot my last week in New York in earnest. This would surely be a send-off to beat all send-offs and we'd dance the night away at Swing 46, Rainbow Room, and Bongo Hut.

At the appointed time, I set out into a drizzly April evening, donned in my finest sport coat, black silk shirt and scarf, my sails all trimmed and shipshape for an evening with a lovely and vivacious lady. Miranda had texted that she'd meet me outside the Jane Hotel on West and Jane Streets. While the West Side Highway zooms with traffic nearby, the sidewalks at that location are not jammed with tourists and pedestrians. It's one of New York's quiet West Village spots overhung with trees, which still had no leaves and were silhouetted against the sky like spindly black hands hovering over me as I approached.

Thinking back, I have to wonder what I would have done had I actually checked to see where the Queen Mary was located on that particular day, which is easily ascertainable on the cruise line's website? Had I done so, I would have had a tingle go up my spine upon learning that the Queen Mary was in fact docked not in Brooklyn but in Southampton, England. Yet why would I have checked such a thing? Was I to proceed through the rest of my life assuming that every sunrise was some sort of deception to draw me outside into the clutches of abductors?

Perhaps so.

A van was parked in the crook where Jane elbows uptown into West Street, and as I drew near, five black men in black berets, black frame glasses and black trench coats piled out of the back. They looked like a band of 50s beatniks.

To many, this sort of gathering might sound alarming, but as a New Yorker, I was used to many unusual people, many of them in groups. So this phalanx of beatniks did not alarm me.

They all faced me.

Politely, I smiled at them and nodded a passing greeting.

Was there ever such a naïve dope as I?

In concert, the black beatniks grabbed me by both shoulders and heaved me into the back of the van, whence I tumbled along a rug until I rolled sideways into the back of the front seats. I felt the beatniks scramble quickly into the back of the darkened van and heard the rear doors slam. The van lurched forward, several of the men shouting excitedly in a foreign tongue that was not European.

In the gloom of the van, I could only see vague shapes and feel the beatniks pressing me into the floor. An accented voice boomed a harsh baritone, commanding: "Don't move, Von Lichtenbichler! We will not harm you unless you compel us to do so."

'Lick-ten-bickler?'

The van swayed violently, the engine racing as the vehicle made its getaway.

There was a sharp pain in my bicep like someone was pinching me, but I quickly recognized the pain as that of a hypodermic needle.

My confusion and panic melted into the miasma of semi-consciousness from whatever drug they had injected into my arm. As slumber's shroud closed in, I recall repeating over and over to myself, like an echo:

Von Lick-ten-bickler...

Von Lick-ten-bickler...

Von Lick-ten-bickler...

CHAPTER 3

CLANG...

   CLANG...

   CLANG...

Those sounds were my first sensation as I regained consciousness. There was also an incessant hissing sound, my skin felt warm and there was a tinny aroma not unlike the smell of a chicken coop. As I fluttered open my eyes, I saw a bright light in front of me. No, it was above me, I was on my back, and the source of the light was a bare bulb on a cracked plaster ceiling. I wasn't sure if I could move, or if I could even try to move. Then my eyes shifted to see that I had just raised my arm, and the bicep on that arm ached. Beyond my arm was a tan plaster wall.

What I was lying on felt like a bed, and I recognized the clanging and hissing as the sounds made by steam heat boilers and radiators.

I listened to the radiators and myself breathing for I'm not sure how long, my eyes squinting at the light bulb. Consciousness was struggling to take full hold of my brain. I heard that accented, baritone voice from the van:

"Is he awake?"

And then an accented woman's voice:

"Lichtenbichler, are you awake?"

All at once I sat up, my panic at being abducted returning in fuller bloom.

I was in a sparse room, sitting up on a cheap single bed. Nothing was on the walls, and the one window opposite me had a metal grate across it, the kind that New Yorkers have in apartments to prevent intruders entering from the fire escape.

The surroundings gave me some measure of hope that I was still in New York – somewhere.

I was further glad to see that my limbs were not bound or handcuffed.

I was also reassured that the two people sitting in folding metal chairs in front of the window were not pointing weapons at me. One on the left was a hefty black man with full features. He still had his beatnik outfit on, and sat backwards on the chair, large arms draped in front of him. At his side sitting front-wise was an equally stocky black woman in a hoodie and black sunglasses.

Big Beatnik said: "He's awake."

"I can see that." She tilted her head at me, and in a lilting voice said: "We can't let you go to Zarenga Chi."

I felt dizzy, yet swung my feet over the side of the bed and onto the floor, putting my head in my hands. I looked down and saw that I was not wearing shoes.

What manner of insanity was this? What had I gotten into now?

There's no doubt that I have been subjected to some fairly substantial horrors since becoming a celebrity. I had seen numerous people killed and actually killed people myself. I had even been abducted, though politely. I had witnessed the results of torture, yet I had not been imprisoned in a way that torture seemed likely. You know, in dungeons or sparse rooms in unknown locations.

Like the one I was in with the beatniks.

This bare bulb room seemed ripe for torture. Above all life's dreads the notion of being helpless and shackled and tormented was something I feared above all else, even temperance. So dampening my desperation and keeping my wits to save my skin required considerable self-control.

I cleared my throat. "Why have I been abducted?"

Big Beatnik: "We know why you are going to Zarenga Chi."

I heaved a weary sigh, the cobwebs in my brain making it difficult to formulate thoughts. "I'm contractually obligated and beholden to Amalgamated

Consumables." I was still looking at my feet – my head felt like I was wearing an iron hat.

She spat: "Lying is ridiculous, Lichtenbichler."

"We are the Zarenga Liberation Front," he boomed. "The people must have a duly elected government. The kingdom cannot be perpetuated at the cost of the populace, and in the favor of the rich who have taken our nation from us."

I finally raised my head, squinting at them and rubbing my temples. If I didn't know better, I would have assumed that these two characters were part of a hip hop act of some kind. "I don't understand what this has to do with me or why you've kidnapped me. And its 'Linsen-bigler,' that's how my name is pronounced. Maybe you think I'm someone else?" I felt surreptitiously with one hand for my phone, but it was in my sport coat and I wasn't wearing a sport coat any longer.

Hoodie Girl said to Big Beatnik: "This is the right guy?"

"Oh, yeah, definitely the cocktail guy. Maybe he don't know?"

"Bullshit," she sneered. "Why would they want someone like him if he wasn't von Lichtenbichler?"

"They hired me to be a spokesman for their beverage brand. I can't see why that is any threat to you. I don't understand." My head was clearing, and I felt as though I might be able to muster some charm – so I produced a pained smile and an air of utter reason. "Really, you've made some sort of mistake, an honest mistake, and I'm willing to forget all about it if you'll just give me my sport coat and call me a cab." *...Straight to the nearest police station.*

She snorted and stood. "Where your father grow up?"

"What?"

"Your father. Where he grow up."

"Altoona, Pennsylvania. Why?"

They said in unison: "You're Lichtenbichler."

I gave my face a good rub. "OK, if I'm who you say I am, why can't you let me go to Zarenga Chi and be a liquor spokesman? How is that going to hurt anything?"

Big Beatnik: "I don't think he knows. And even if he do, when we explain, he has to face the truth."

"Look, guys, I implore you." I put my hands together as if invoking prayer. "Can't we go somewhere and discuss this over a drink? I'm a reasonable man. If you tell me what this is all about, and it's plain that my going to Zarenga Chi is wrong, well, I of course won't go. I'm a man of honor."

Hoodie Girl: "Honorable man that blows up fish."

I kept smiling, ignoring the comment. "Look, I mean, what are you going to do with me – just hold me forever? Kill me? You look like honest people, who are very sincere about their Liberation Front of Zarenga."

They said in unison: "Zarenga Liberation Front."

I pointed at them. "See? You have the name down pat and everything. You have to believe me, I'm no threat to anyone, and if you feel I shouldn't go, I won't go, let's just cut right to the chase. It must be true and good if you felt this strongly to abduct me like this."

Hoodie Girl: "We need you for propaganda. Here."

She nudged Big Beatnik and handed me a piece of note paper printed in block letters. I squinted at it. Lately, reading glasses had become increasingly necessary, yet I'd been resistant to succumbing to a frailty of middle age. So I was having trouble making out what the note said both for lack of reading glasses and a blurring, drugged mind.

Big Beatnik pointed his phone at me and boomed: "Look into the camera and read the note."

I waved the note paper. "Is this a ransom demand?" I had been forced to do that once before in the Bahamas. "If it is I can ad lib. Just tell me the amount."

I heard loud thumping in the other room – someone pounding on a door?

"Open up!" a woman's voice shouted. "FBI."

There was scuffling in the other room – I would guess it was the rest of the black beatniks. Big Beatnik jumped to his feet, eyes wild, and threw himself on the window gates, struggling to open them.

Hoodie Girl suddenly had a small revolver in her hand, at her waist, and it was pointed at me.

"We can't let him get away. We cannot let him go to Zarenga Chi!"

I've done my share of heroics and then some – largely inadvertently, mind you. I had yet, however, to fling myself on someone pointing a gun at me. The odds of avoiding serious injury by going towards instead of away from a loaded gun seemed unfavorable. I'm no gun expert by any means, but from what little experience I had with handguns, I knew they tended to be wildly inaccurate even at short range. I felt my best chances were to increase distance. And by 'felt' I mean exactly that – there was no time for any calculus. My shrewd ploy, in short was to run away, an old standby of mine.

I dove away from her across the bed as the gun fired. The slug went *PANG* on the metal bedframe.

I rolled off the other side of the bed onto the floor. Was I hit?

I heard the window grate fly open and hit the wall with a metallic *BANG*

Then glass shattered and another two shots, different from the first one.

Big Beatnik shrieked and I heard him fall to the floor like a sack of mangoes.

There was commotion in the next room as the FBI rammed open the front door to the apartment. "ON THE GROUND!"

Someone was smashing out the window in the bedroom, glass and splinters skittering across the floor. A shadow was cast over me, someone breathing heavily.

A husky voice said: "Are you OK, Mr. Linsenbigler?"

I rolled over and looked up at the silhouette of a man in body armor holding an F16 or some such. He had a helmet emblazoned: FBI. Behind him, I could see where he had smashed his way in through the window from the fire escape.

All I could think to say was: "Am I bleeding?"

"A little."

"Did she shoot me?"

"Maybe a little."

"A little?"

CHAPTER 4

A LITTLE?

In the head, to be exact.

Hoodie Girl had fired a little .38 slug that ricocheted off the bed frame and directly through the upper scapha of my right ear. You could see daylight through the hole, which was about the diameter of a pencil.

I suppose the bright side of this new deformity was that it was on the opposite side of my head from the small 'x' scar under my left eye – the one I got in a sword fight.

I had been shuttled by the FBI in their tactical SUVs to Jamaica Hospital, which is in a neighborhood of that name in Queens, New York. My abductors had held me in a second story apartment just off Liberty Avenue and next to a live halal poultry market, thus the chicken coop smell.

Both Hoodie Girl and Big Beatnik had been shot by the agent who came in from the fire escape. She was dead, Big Beatnik was in surgery, and the rest of the beatnik gang had been arrested.

The FBI's timely recue had yet to be explained to me as I was escorted to a black van by a cluster of agents, the top of my right ear smartly topped with a wad of bright white bandages. They had recovered my cell phone and wallet, which were in my sport coat slung over my shoulder.

Inside the back of the van was a cluster of inner facing leather-bound chairs – it looked comfy and was dimly lit like the back of a limousine. Three of the chairs were occupied – one most strikingly by an older gentleman in a pinstripe suit and flowing white hair fronted by kindly wrinkles and round wire specs. He beckoned me to enter and take the seat between him and a stately black man in a seersucker suit and carnation. Opposite them was a woman in rimless glasses and a crew cut hacking away at the keys to a computer in her lap. She didn't look up as I climbed cautiously into the van and settled into my seat.

The old man nodded at me, and croaked in a gravelly, southern drawl: "Mr. Linsenbigler, my name is Linus Trimble, with the Justice Department, and I am a mind reader."

I pinched the bridge of my nose. Wasn't it enough that I had already gone through a drugging and abduction and gun ballet that I now had to be given some sort of song and dance about why? Did it matter, really? Nobody needed to explain anything to me that ultimately

I did not already know, which was that I was for some reason being dragged into some other insane situation. "Can I please just go back to my hotel and have this chat tomorrow?"

He ignored my comment. "And when I read your mind, this is what it was thinking."

I heard the siren song of ice tinkling in a glass, and detected the whiff of corn mash. The old man held out an etched tumbler of whisky. He said: "I know you no longer care for Pappy Van Winkle after your time in Guatemala, though I'm not sure I could have scared that up in a single evening. I know that you like wheated bourbon for Manhattans, and rye-forward bourbons on cold nights. However, I didn't fuss too much, knowing also that you sometimes favor any drink rather than none. I prefer Tennessee whiskies, so in deference to my own tastes and proclivities, this is a glass of George Dickel Sour Mash. I do hope it suffices."

The van began to move, and I could see headlights and taillights of adjoining cars dimly through the van's tinted glass.

I took the glass and saw that he had one of his own, which he swirled and pointed at the black gentleman on my other side. "This is Mr. Noomba, the Zarenga Chi ambassador. He doesn't drink as a matter of religious imperative. I will defer to him to impart the particulars of the reason you were abducted."

Mr. Noomba nodded deeply, and raised an eyebrow at me. "Let me be the first to supply profound apologies for the actions of these terrorists from my island nation, and assure you that this is an aberration. Zarenga Chi, a nation in good standing with the United Nations and the African League of Nations, is indebted to the United States diligence in tracking these people and their quick and decisive action to intercede to both rescue you and terminate this terrorist cell. Within the borders of Zarenga Chi, our own police and investigators have amply tracked and eradicated cells of this group. Outside our borders, we have limited control over what they do. It is only through the utmost spirit of cooperation among all nations to assist each other in halting the advance of all terrorist groups throughout our world. That you have been drawn unwittingly into this conflict and been injured means that you have also served in this fight against evil, and in fact been instrumental in facilitating the dismantling of this terrorist cell, and I am authorized to award you our nation's Cross of Valor, also known as The Lichtenbichler Cross."

Noomba held out a palm-size leather case, and his mahogany fingers delicately peeled back the lid. Resting on a bed of black velvet was a red enameled gold cross on a chain. The cross was small enough to fill the palm of your hand.

My glass was empty and I rattled the ice at Trimble. "Linus, are you still reading my mind?"

He chuckled and refilled my glass as I admired the cross in the dim light. I shook my head and said: "Mr. Noomba, this is an honor, but I really can't accept this, I didn't do anything. Perhaps I was a catalyst...wait, you said this was the Cross of Lichtenbichler? I'm confused. My kidnappers used that pronunciation, but my name is Lin-sen-bigler."

Noomba nodded deeply again as I sipped my second glass of sour mash. "Maximillian Von Lichtenbichler is the liberator and father of our nation, much like your George Washington."

Somehow I'd missed this in my reading, though I had not focused on history, but more on geography and fishing. Our van slipped onto the Van Wyck Expressway, the lights of other cars swirling around us dimly through the tinted windows.

I squinted at Noomba: "These beatniks were saying ...hey, why were they dressed as beatniks, anyway?"

He blinked slowly, as though pained to have to explain. "These terrorists consider themselves liberators, and they wear berets as a display of unity when committing crimes. No doubt they were telling you that our people are oppressed. Nothing could be farther from the truth."

"I know that Zarenga Chi has a very high standard of living. But that's another thing, why were they calling me Lichtenbichler?"

Linus's voice growled to life: "They think you are related to their founding father and that you are going to Zarenga Chi to support the monarchy."

I turned to him, and he raised his eyes from his glass. "Boone, it appears that you are distantly related."

Noomba chimed in: "Zarenga was an obscure part of an 1888 acquisition by the German East Africa Company. The Sultan of Zanzibar leased his East Africa holdings to the Germans. On mainland Africa, this resulted in the Abushiri revolt, which was instigated by the indigenous Arab elite. Zarenga, however, welcomed the Germans, who ousted cruel Arab plantation owners. Maximillian Von Lichtenbichler was the administrator who had been sent to govern Zarenga, and he instituted land reforms that promulgated greater production of aromatic plants like ylang-ylang, frangipani, jasmine, lemongrass and vanilla. As such, the natives prospered along with the German East Africa Company.

Lichtenbichler was the bastard child of Bavaria's King Ludwig III's and borne to an unidentified Viennese dynast of his late cousin Archduchess Mathilde of Austria. At that time, a child out of wedlock was placed in the care of foster parents who were compensated for raising him. As such, the child took the last name of those who raised him. The largesse of his Viennese birth mother ensured that he attended good schools and attained a commission in the Bavarian Army. And so it was that after serving as a captain in the cavalry and distinguishing himself as a swordsman and founder of the Bavarian Balloon Detachment, he was recruited by the East Africa Company to manage the affairs of Zarenga Chi as a German colony."

"Wait wait wait." I interrupted. "Bavarian Balloon Detachment?" *Didn't they open for Hot Tuna once?*

Noomba looked mystified that I would find this curious. "Maximillian was an avid aeronaut. He introduced ballooning to Zarenga. It is a very popular sport even today in our nation. At any rate, to continue, Zarenga was an obscure portion of German East Africa, so much so that the Treaty of Versailles following World War One failed to account for it when dividing German territories in Africa. Some say that because it began with a 'z' that it fell off the bottom of the list. Zarenga was no longer a German colony, nor was it anybody else's colony, and it was then that Zarengis realized that they were their own country. Von Lichtenbichler was becoming old by that time, but he was revered. He had in effect been running the nation as an omnipotent ruler, and so he was formally decreed king in a manifesto endorsed by a consortium of plantation managers who instituted a congress from among their ranks to advise the king and those kings to follow. This system remains today, as does a commitment to provide our citizens with one of the highest standards of living anywhere."

I finished my second drink just as Noomba finished his history lesson. "I see. But, um, aren't many of your citizens imported. That is, like the employees of corporations that have located there. Or me – I'm now a Zarengi and have dual citizenship."

Noomba's brow wrinkled, briefly. "This is true, but the natives have also prospered. They have free schooling, college and health care."

"Well, if everything is so great for the natives, why is there a Liberation Front of Zarenga? "

"Zarengi Liberation Front," Linus corrected. "ZLF."

Noomba smirked. "It is said that in any organization or nation, one percent of the people create ninety-nine percent of the problems. These terrorists are the one percent. Instead of going to school and becoming a part of the economy, they have instead chosen to criticize and feel that money should just be handed to them. Believe me, when you come to your new country, you will see that we have no slums. Some live simply in the traditional style out of choice."

I couldn't help wonder where exactly the truth in all this really was. As just about anybody knows by now, one man's terrorist is another's freedom fighter. It sounded to me as if the truth might be that the natives had become a servant class to all the fat cats that had moved in – that certainly seemed to be what the ZLF beatniks were on about.

One thing was for sure: Linus was an operator, in a league with others I'd met, in Russia, in particular. He was a manipulator. He was there to compel me to do something I didn't want to do. It was only a matter of time before I found out what that was.

"Trimble? Noomba? There's something you both need to understand. I am non-political. I choose to remain politically neutral here in The States and beyond. So if anybody has designs on Boone Linsenbigler contributing to propaganda, that is clearly outside my contractual obligations to Amalgamated Consumables."

Linus chuckled deep in his chest, squinting at me. "Who said anything about propaganda?"

I smirked at him. "I may not be political, but that doesn't mean I can't understand people's motives. The ZLF wanted me to do propaganda for their side, and I can see that since I might be related to Lick-ten-bickler that I might be used to help prop up the monarchy in some way."

Noomba clucked his tongue, objecting. "Zarenga Chi is not in need of any propping, I assure you. That does not mean, however, that we don't take measures to avoid bad publicity or allow the ZLF any encouragement, which is why we'd like to keep this episode and your abduction quiet."

I jerked a thumb at Trimble. "If he can manage it on his end, I certainly don't want to be at the center of this controversy in any way."

Noomba smiled, faintly. "Excellent. If you are amenable, Zarenga Chi would like to take the precaution of avoiding any further attempts on your person, or draw any possible media attention, and transport you immediately by government sponsored transport to our nation and to your employer, Amalgamated Consumables. As I said, we feel we have better control of the ZLF there than here, and the FBI has participated generously in our nation's fight on terrorism."

Trimble cleared his throat. "The Justice Department stands ready to assist Zarenga Chi and any nation in the war on terror as it manifests itself on U.S. soil."

There was nothing keeping me in New York, especially inasmuch as Miranda was not in town. "When do I leave?"

Linus patted his belly. "We collected your things from the hotel, and Zarenga Chi paid your hotel bill. You leave tonight." He handed me my U.S. and Zarenga Chi passports. "Have a safe trip."

I pursed my lips in thought, and cocked an eyebrow at him. "And Miranda?"

"Miranda?"

"The ZLF knew enough to text me pretending to be a girl I met aboard the Queen Mary a couple of months back. They lured me to the Jane Street Hotel as pretext for having dinner with Miranda. How did they know about her?"

His brow knit. "That I don't know."

A glance at Noomba found him in full shrug.

As far as I knew, the only group who knew about my assignation with Miranda was the U.S. intelligence people who'd gotten me into that mess back in Russia, the ones who claimed to work for the Commerce Department. Were they involved with this? Why would they help the ZLF abduct me? So that it could appear that I subdued them, earned the Cross of Valor?

In fly fishing, there's a technique for catching trout called dead drifting. A fly on very fine, transparent leader is set adrift either atop the water or below in such a way that it appears unattached to any fishing line and so looks completely natural. If the fly drags or flinches, the trout see that it is not moving naturally and will not eat the fly.

I just saw the fly twitch.

CHAPTER 5

WHISKED THROUGH SECURITY and into a charter terminal, I was escorted deftly onto an airliner and into a private cabin.

The kind of airline cabin you see in the ads for the fancy airlines that give you a bed.

The kind you know you're never going to be able to afford.

It was a little longer than three portholes, and as wide as the usual three seats across. Inside was a plush leather built-in easy chair facing a flat screen that had a walnut computer shelf in front of it. The chair obviously converted into a bed. A low shelf at the window was also walnut and had a minibar built into the wall under it. Cone lamps with brown lampshades lit the corners of the room.

The stark comparison between what lay before me and the previous twenty-five years of crush in commercial airlines made part of me want to weep with gratitude.

It was also the kind of airliner with young, attractive 'stewardesses.' No, not 'flight attendants,' whose current standard bearer could resemble your Mom or your Dad. Nothing wrong with that, but I'd rather have the former, all things considered.

As such, I was led to my little state room by a petite black stewardess in a tight blue skirt, heels and low-cut teal tunic revealing delightful cleavage. Her caramel skin fairly glowed, and her eyes were bright blue above a button nose and pouty red lips. Her smile was bright, but her demeanor ever so sly in the way those blue eyes inspected mine. "Welcome aboard Zarenga Airlines, Mr. Linsenbigler. I trust we can make your flight to our capital city Nambia an enjoyable one. My name is Foresh. Can I get you a cocktail?"

The sly manner and the way she spoke it was almost as if she was being facetious, as if at any second she was going to laugh in my face and drag me to economy seating. Perhaps it was her accent or the lilt in her voice that was throwing me off.

Ever one to embrace the moment, I made a show of surveying my quarters dispassionately as though it was adequate. I smoothed my slender mustache, favored her with a blithe smile and said: "Vodka martini, up, mixed dry with white wine, not vermouth, and a double twist."

She cocked her head and touched a finger to her lower lip. "As you wish, though during take-off, watch that your martini doesn't spill, you know, should the aircraft move up and down abruptly."

I raised an eyebrow. By gads, I do believe she was flirting with me! "Foresh, I've been through many take-offs and landings, with lots of up and down movements. The trick is to embrace the glass firmly, yet carefully, and work it gradually until cruising altitude."

We savored a pause as she suppressed a fuller smile, the eyes flashing. "Let me shake one up for you, Mr. Linsenbigler."

Foresh turned, and swayed down the hallway, her long brown hair brushing her bottom as she went.

Mind you, there I was, a man who had just been drugged and wounded in a chicken coop shootout not hours before, and here I was back on my steed as if I had not just been thrown willy-nilly from the saddle. Behold the enduring miracle of testosterone!

For those acquainted with my romantic forays, they know these exploits come in all stripes. Like any man, I am an opportunist when it comes to the ladies, but do have the ability to turn tail should the lady in question seem certifiably insane. Mostly. A select few are mysterious as to motive. However, I am not clairvoyant and do not feel obligated to try to discern which are genuinely attracted to me and which have been, shall we say, provided for me. It seemed possible that Foresh had been provided to make my flight extra enjoyable, and that posh airlines with private cabins might have special amenities. Inasmuch as there was no way of knowing, my imperative, as always, was *carpe diem*.

I am keen not to overplay my hand, a *faux pas* much discouraged in our times, and rightly so. Flirting is not an open invitation. That is why my *modus operandi* it to flirt until the lady makes the first, overtly coy move.

Compelling a fish to take the fly willingly requires temptation and a natural presentation. Temptation is appetite, and either it's there or it isn't, but if it is, there's a chance. Presenting the fly to the fish needs to be done in a way that places the morsel in front of the fish so that it does not look false or like a trap. So if a girl flirts she is letting you know she has appetite and is tempted. Excuses to innocently touch her hand or face or body constitutes a natural presentation leading up to a kiss or more.

The cabin did not have a bathroom – that was down the hall along with a shower. My cabin had a small sink and mirror, complete with various toiletries. Inspecting myself in the mirror, I carefully removed the large white bandage from atop my ear, revealing the pea-sized hole speckled with the remains of antiseptic mercurochrome. The wound was not bleeding, and I dabbed it dry before applying a smaller bandage strip. A much more presentable Boone grinned at me from the mirror.

"This is your captain speaking," came over a speaker under the flat screen. "Please prepare for departure. Take your seats, upright them and fasten your seat belts. Your attendant will check to see you are prepared."

I took my seat, and as I fastened my seat belt, Foresh arrived, glistening martini in hand. She swiveled and did a patented bunny dip to place the glass on the drink console next to the window. She scowled at me, waving a finger: "I'm going to come back at altitude and check to make sure you haven't spilled that martini."

"I would hope so. And what if I have spilled?"

She grinned, and before closing the door, said: "That means you really aren't that good at the up and down part as you think you are."

Blast. I wondered whether she was just flirting as part of her job the way some barmaids do. Well, tally that up to the indomitable optimism of men when confronted with sexual prospects.

As we taxied, the captain explained that we had two stops along the way, the first in Frankfurt some eight hours on, and the other in Dubai, another seven, and then another five to our final destination. Of course, because of date lines, that would put me in Nambia the following morning.

I finished the martini before we reached the runway, and was fast asleep by the time the wheels left the ground.

So much for the miracle of testosterone.

I awoke slowly some hours later to the sound of a gentle snore that was not mine. For a moment, I flashed back to awaking in that chicken coop in Jamaica, to the clang I heard when I awoke, wondering if I were back there or whether none of the previous day had happened at all. Kidnapped by beatniks?

Sun shone through the airline window onto my eyelids not too unlike that light bulb on the ceiling.

The whine of the airliner's engines confirmed for me that I was indeed on the Zarenga Airlines flight to Nambia.

I had fallen asleep sitting up but my chair had been folded down into a bed and I was lying on my side toward the window. A wiggle of my toes told me my shoes had been removed, just as they had in Jamaica. The similarities to my abduction were sort of startling.

Yet that was not the clang of a radiator but a gentle snore, the kind that sounds like faraway lawn mowers cutting summer grass. It wasn't me snoring...

I rolled over to see Foresh tucked in next to me, her head draped in the long chocolate hair and the little nose smooshed into the pillow. Her scent, which did not seem like perfume, was of a ripe apple freshly bitten. A blanket was clutched around her.

Foresh's uniform hung by a hanger on the back of the door.

Now what the devil was I to make of this? Checking my memory banks, I was dashed certain that I had not parried and thrust the night before, and I was still clothed. So she just took the liberty of sacking out with me? A glance at the flat screen revealed that it was displaying the progress of the flight, and I could see that the graphic of our plane was at the coast of Ireland. A rough guess told me that a landing in Frankfurt was likely less than two hours off.

I sat up and liberated a cola from the minibar – not my breakfast beverage of choice but sugar and caffeine were required.

Puzzling over the girl in my bed, I decided to wake her and get some sense of whether this was an indication of better things to come. I mean, she's crawled in bed with me, what more did I need to know? But the mixed signals from the night before made me uncertain. She had an odd way about her and her inflection made everything she said sound like an insinuation when perhaps it was not.

Grasping the curve of her calf, I gave it a gentle squeeze. "Foresh? It's morning."

She sat up suddenly, her hair rolling off her head, and the blanket dropping to expose her caramel breasts haltered in a bright pink lace bra. "What time is it?"

"Little after eight."

She blinked her big blue puffy eyes at me and grinned. "I have to go to work."

Rolling off the bed, the blanket fell to the floor as she stood, her pert bottom fetchingly contained in matching pink panties. Below that were black stockings.

Raise the mizzen sails, Old Man, steady as she goes!

In a trice she had wiggled back into her skirt and was buttoning her tunic. "You want coffee, Mr. Linsenbigler?"

Coffee? Furthest thing from my mind just then. "I dare say that inasmuch as we've been bunk mates, you can call me Boone." Indeed, after the quick tour of her lingerie and physique, she could call me just about anything.

She swept her hair up in both hands, twisted it rapidly and then clipped it into a bun with a claw clip from her pocket. At the mirror, she glossed her lips with a wand from the other pocket, then set about brushing mascara on her lashes. "We're not supposed to call the customers by their first names, Mr. Linsenbigler. What kind of breakfast would you like?"

Flopping back into bed but into a sitting position, I folded my arms and cocked my head at her. "I would imagine, Foresh, that you're also not supposed to sleep with the customers – not that I mind."

"All the cabins are filled and the attendants don't have beds, just reclining chairs. So when I found you asleep, I tucked you in, and then shared. You really don't mind?" With a flourish she dusted her cheeks with blush, and turned toward me, blinking rapidly as if to elicit my answer.

"I'd mind less if you came by while I was conscious and we could share a couple of cocktails before bed, maybe a snack, get acquainted. My father said: *Never sleep with strangers unless you've eaten pie together.*"

She squinted at me. "I don't think we have any pie."

"I'm sure there must be some sort of substitute aboard – my father was forever speaking figuratively." Figuratively? I was being generous. Most of his sayings made little or no sense at all.

She put a hand on the doorknob as she stepped into her high heels. "OK. How do you want your eggs?"

"Easy over, with bacon and toast."

"What kind of toast? Or English muffin?"

"Surprise me."

She opened the door quickly and as she rolled around the door and into the hall she smirked at me. "I just might."

Never before or since have I seen a woman rise from bed, dress, adjust her makeup and depart with such alacrity. I think she did it in less than a minute and a half.

CHAPTER 6

"THIS IS YOUR CAPTAIN SPEAKING."

We had just parked at our gate in Frankfurt, the plane flanked by Lufthansa aircraft with round yellow logos on their tails. I know the shape in that yellow circle is supposed to be a bird but I can't help seeing it as a flying fork.

My breakfast had been brought to me not by Foresh but by another stewardess, and the decimated tray was on the floor by the door.

The Captain continued: "On behalf of the crew, we thank you for flying Zarenga Air. We've timed out our maximum flight time, so please stand by as we board new passengers and switch crews. Enjoy the remainder of your flight."

Dash it all – that would mean Foresh would not be continuing on. I could still smell her apple-like scent on the pillow and had been looking forward to getting better acquainted.

Once in the air again, a rather prim black stewardess came to take my tray and see if I needed anything. One couldn't imagine that this one wore hot pink lingerie. I indicated an iced tea would be welcome, and she left.

While the poshness of the private cabin was certainly desirable over the alternative, I felt a wee bit isolated. Yet there were no communal spaces on the plane. As such, I was relegated to the flat screen to pass the time. I am not much of a movie buff, not of the endless series of explosions that are passed off as entertainment nowadays. Then again, one has a completely different perspective of this sort of drama when you have indeed been in similar situations yourself. The gunplay and crashes and eruptions of fire make me cringe.

So Boone Linsenbigler, Fearless American Hero, winced as he flipped through channel after channel of hyper-violent cinema. One alternative was numbing retreads of nuclear family yuk-em-up sitcoms. Another was war documentaries, which not as violent as the superhero movies, were depressing. As much as my wits had saved my hide from various dangers, I would fare poorly in actual battle. There's no talking or hiding or sneaking or drinking or fishing your way out of hand to hand combat. True enough, I'd fought and killed by sword two men. I was lucky – one was rash and the other old.

In the mirror I inspected the wound to my ear again and it did not seem infected and it did not hurt unless touched. It was a clean pink circle through my right upper ear lobe. The hospital said the hole could be filled by plastic surgery, though it did balance the small 'x' dueling scar under my left eye – together interesting conversation pieces and for better or worse a testament to my derring-do. *Boone a phony? Lookie here! How many dueling scars and bullet holes do you have, Naysaying Bloggers?*

When they gathered my things from the hotel room, they had the presence of mind to pack me a travel bag, which I opened and inspected the contents. My shaving kit was there, so I scraped off facial hair here and there, but with cognition that I was trying now to grow out my whiskers to their former glory.

I donned a simple change of clothes, to include gray lounging pants and V-neck sweater.

Also contained in the bag was the stack of sport fishing magazines I'd collected from newsstands in Manhattan, a find that caused me to gasp with pleasure. Here was something to do with the time sequestered in my private cabin!

Of most interest to me was an article on fly fishing for wahoo, a toothy fish with extremely dangerous maw that put barracuda to shame. Slender like 'cuda and around four to six feet long, they are silver with blue tiger striping on their backs. Their teeth are literally like four serrated knife blades. Their eyes are small, yellow and malevolent. 'Hoo' are powerful in the extreme, so much so that if brought aboard alive they have been known to thrash and slash and mercilessly wound anybody nearby.

Most people consider fly fishing the delicate sport of deftly flying loops of line in the air. At the end of the line is a willowy clear leader that lands a tiny bug-like fly on a silvery stream surface. The resultant mercurial blister on the water signals the fish has sipped the fly. The fight lasts a couple of minutes before you gently net the fish, free it from the dainty little wire hook, and release the trout back to its cozy little lair behind a rock. The hush of wilderness once more envelops you.

Wahoo must be beaten to death with an aluminum baseball bat to land them. The flies are flashy, usually with two large stainless steel hooks. 'Hoo attack the fly so savagely that you need steel leaders and shock tippets, because once on – assuming they don't cut straight through the line – they run and you cannot stop them. To keep a wahoo from ripping all the line off your reel, you have to fire up the motor and chase after them.

Wahoo are to trout what rugby is to tiddlywinks; what heavy metal is to Bach; what barrel-proof whiskey is to elderberry wine.

Wahoo are arguably the most challenging fish to hook, fight and land on a fly. I felt up to this challenge, and what angler would not want to have accomplished this feat, to have embraced this adventure in angling?

There were also articles on the poorly-named but prized milkfish, which could hardly be more diametrically opposed to wahoo.

Instead of looking like a beady-eyed homicidal maniac, milkfish have the over-sized, incredulous eyes of cartoon minnow. They are silver and white.

Instead of razor-sharp jaws, they have small, toothless lips.

Instead of attacking prey ferociously, they are spooked by any movement of the fly, preferring the lure to look like a pitifully small dead something floating aimlessly in the current.

Instead of cruising in forty fathoms of deep blue, these piteous-looking creatures school aimlessly near shore, sometimes munching on algae like cows at pasture.

Apparently, once hooked, they fight well. To look at them, it is hard to imagine that to be so. No doubt my lack of enthusiasm about these seemingly listless creatures is unfounded, and colored by the drama of hunting 'hoo.

Giant trevally would be another fish to target in Zarenga. Like permit in the Atlantic Ocean, they cruise flats looking for crustaceans and baitfish, sometimes in schools, and fly presentations have to be aggressive to get them to take. The idea is to make your fly look like food trying to escape – that excites them to hit. They are usually less than three feet long, oval and husky, with silver sides and dark speckled backs. Like the wahoo, these are not timid fish, and have the reputation of being very strong fighters, though they do not jump. Because they are usually hunted in shallow water, any kind of debris or plants or rocks or coral on the bottom pose a hazard because they will wrap the line on these and break you off. Wahoo, conversely, are hunted in open water, and their teeth are the main cause of line cuts.

Dorado (Mahi Mahi) would be at hand. I had caught this colorful yellow and blue fish in Baja Sur and they are a favorite of mine. They jump mightily.

Then there would be marlin and sailfish, which I had seen and cast to incidentally but not hooked and landed. Most people are familiar with what these fish look like, and even their great leaping fights.

By early afternoon I had read quite a few articles and at thirty-five thousand feet was chomping at the bit to go fishing. I wondered how long it would be after arrival when I would be able to charter a boat and set upon the seas in search of big game.

There was a gentle knock at my door, and I assumed that it would be my new flight attendant.

To my surprise, it was Foresh. She was not in her uniform but in tight black slacks and sweater that revealed her midriff.

On her feet were slippers.

In her one hand was a bottle of champagne and two flutes. In the other, a tray of cheese, fruit and bread.

"Am I too early?" she said coyly.

I held open the door and she drifted past me into my cabin.

I cleared my throat. "I thought you had disembarked in Frankfurt with the rest of the crew?"

"Obviously not." She shrugged, unwrapping the cork by the light of the portholes. "You see, my week is over, and I am going back to Zarenga Chi. I'm off duty, Boone."

Pop!

"I see. Well, it certainly would be a shame to have to fly all the rest of the way to Zarenga Chi in a coach seat."

"There's a cabin available, vacated in Frankfurt, so I don't have to stay here if you don't want me to." She handed me a glass of bubbly. "Am I being too forward?"

I admired the pale yellow wine and strings of tiny bubbles up the side.

Then I admired her. "Forward? I should say not. Companionable is the right word, and not too much so. Why not be companionable when there's the two of us with nothing to do for thousands of miles?"

She sipped her champagne and beamed at me, her belly button peeking seductively at me from her midriff. "Let's play Denge Chippo!"

Once again I was unsure if she were indeed being seductive or just friendly. "Denge Chippo?" Pronounced *Dengay Chippo*.

"It's on the flat screen. Here, I'll show you."

And so in short order, it was revealed to me that you could play a board game on the flat screen, and this particular one I can only characterize as being like Monopoly or perhaps Life. You roll the dice and your game piece moves the requisite number of squares until you land on one that tells you you've inherited a cassava plantation, a typhoon blew away your village, you're rescued from a desert island and get a book deal, you marry a second spouse (they have monetary value), you have kids (the boys do, the girls do not), the volcano blows up and so on in that manner. Along the way you collect money to buy oil rigs, plantations, ports or bauxite mines – all with a monetary value. The game ends when one player collects three island cards (meaning you've bought an island), which can be purchased from your possessions or by drawings certain cards from a pile on the board. With game pieces at the starting square, we began to roll the dice using a game console I had assumed was merely a TV remote.

As we played Denge Chippo over the next hour or so I intermittently struck up conversation. During that time, she attained an oil rig and a persimmon plantation and I had a port and a fleet of tankers.

"So, Foresh, you're Zarengian?"

"Of course!"

"Born and raised?"

"On the island of Ratupa."

"What was that like, Foresh?"

"What do you mean?"

"Was it a fishing village, what kind of house did you live in, did you go to school?"

'My father had a vanilla plantation, a small one, and we had a house on a rise near the ocean. School is required. I wore a uniform with a skirt up to here, drove the boys crazy."

"How did you end up in this line of work?"

"College."

"Vocational college?"

She knit her brow at me, clearly not understanding. "College is college."

"What I meant was, you could have studied anything there and perhaps become a botanist or lawyer…"

"College did not have those. Mostly it's hospitality for women. Men – electrical and plumbing and airport work."

"Did you ever wish you had studied those other things, or had an opportunity like that?"

She shrugged, looking at me like I was crazy. "No. This is a good job. I travel, meet interesting people like you. Then I have my home near Nambia Beach. I like to swim and snorkel."

"Do you fish?"

"Spear fish, sometimes. Mostly I collect lobster."

"I do a lot of fishing, but with a fly rod."

"What's a fly rod?" She put a finger to her lip, and laughed. "You catch flying fish with it?"

"Not yet! Fly fishing is with a rod and reel, you just have to throw the line in the air first."

"Oh, yes, I see them do this sometime. Very curious. I never knew it was called flies fishing." She nudged me playfully with her shoulder. "You take me fishing, show me how to fly with fishes?"

"I'd be delighted, Foresh."

"What's it like being famous, Boone?"

"You've heard of me?"

She laughed. "Everybody in Zarenga Chi has heard of you by now."

"Really?"

"Oh, yes. Amalgamated Consumables has made your arrival well known. So is it fun being famous? They are flying you in this luxury class, that must be fun! Do you have a chauffeur and a butler? And when it snows do you wear furs from animals? That must be very strange."

Now I had to laugh. "Foresh, being famous is not all that fun. The money is nice. Maybe some people think it's fun. For me? I am not any kind of hero – that's just what they made me out to be."

She looked askance at me, knitting her brow. "They show on TV you sword fighting and killing a man, in a very dangerous place. I see you in Russia dancing on a train with swords with snow all around. I see you dancing on a fancy ship in fancy clothes with a beautiful woman. You throw explosives to kill big fish! Maybe you are not a hero, but you have a very exciting life. What happened to your ear?"

"I cut it accidentally. It's nothing."

"The girls, they must throw themselves at you." She rolled the dice and blushed ever so slightly. Maybe one bit your ear?"

"Foresh, I may be famous, but believe it or not I don't play Denge Chippo with just anybody." I brushed her hair from her face, and she smiled. "Ah look there, you've landed on an island square!"

Foresh clapped her hands and used a newly acquired bauxite mine, an airstrip, a husband and two sons to buy a small island.

"Ah, Boone, now you will see a very interesting way to play Denge Chippo." With that she removed her top and slacks, and there were those lovely brown breasts in the pink bra, and her honeyed brown bottom in lacy pink panties. "Anytime you buy an island you have to take off layer of clothing. I said I would surprise you and I did!"

Nodding, I deftly reached for and opened the second bottle of champagne.

Now we're getting somewhere.

I would have cheated to make me land on the next island space but the electronic game wouldn't let you do that, it moved your piece for you. Lo and behold, I drew a card that sent me to an island space.

Me: black boxer briefs.

She: pink lingerie.

Vexingly, island spaces eluded us while we each acquired further properties and incurred other fines and actions completely unrelated to the removal of clothing. And there within reach her silky curves fairly shimmered.

Ay yi yi, Monopoly was never like this when I was a kid.

To that point, Foresh just seemed like a kid having fun, laughing and yelping with each new surprise in the game, seemingly oblivious that she was nearly naked.

Sure enough, she landed once more on an island space and had two islands to my one.

She stood, dropped her bra, her brown orbs of delight bouncing, the tight brown nipples staring back at me. She wiggled out of her panties, revealing a most fetchingly trimmed V of delight and the base of her taught russet tummy.

I laughed with her on this turn of events (albeit with a slight quaver of suppressed lust), and asked: "So what happens if you get three islands and win? You'll have no other clothes, precious."

"If I win, the game is over and you have to please me."

Please her? I let it go without further details, figuring I would find out soon enough.

However, as it turned out, I acquired my second island in short order. Now we were both naked, and she pointed at my formidables and laughed: "Oh, very nice, you trim nice, too. We have a matching set!"

So now you know – I believe grooming extends beyond the neck and nails. That may seem fussy, but in all honesty, who wants to be the intrepid sexual explorer who has to hack his or her way through a jungle of hair to reveal the Golden City?

I further digress to reflect upon interesting intimate interludes I've had in the past. Like the Japanese provider in Nassau and her artful full-body massage that was sex that was not sex. And who could forget the homicidal Russian redhead in a steam bath in the snows of Siberia whipping my torso with eucalyptus branches. Couplings of those sorts were not beyond the pale. But this? Monopoly sex on an airliner?

Foresh landed on an island space and giggled.

She did not even bother to trade her palm oil plant and desalination plant in to make her purchase.

Instead, she raised up from the bed and lowered the window shades, the curve of her bottom enchantingly cocked to one side. The cabin was cast in a sultry light. She turned back toward me, clicking off the game.

Wriggling her lithe caramel body all the way back into my lounger, hair tossed over half her face, she drew one shapely leg over the other, coyly hiding her puss.

She bit a finger and whispered: "You have to please me, Boone."

As Boone Linsenbigler, Master Cocktailer and an erstwhile pillar of probity, I am duty bound to be a gentleman even when succumbing to baser instincts.

A grandee does not kiss and tell.

However, I think it has been amply demonstrated that I am not who I pretend to be, and it would be unseemly at this juncture to simply give you a wink and close the door.

As to my obligation to please Foresh, I will divulge that, given my normal proclivities, my policy is always ladies first, so this turn of events was standard operating procedure.

And I will further note – as much a point of principle as anything else – that some women find their breasts true erogenous zones and others less so. Foresh was of the first camp, and yet so many men fail miserably at the art of mammary caress. *Caress,* you idiots – don't just dive in at the nipples like Fido on a squeaky chew toy. The outer sides of the breast are particularly sensitive to gentle, erotic strokes, and it is essential to build anticipation for participation by the lips and tongue as you circle inwards to the teat. Apologies for proselytizing, but the mishandling of glorious breasts is really a travesty of the first order. Go and sin no more.

Yet for all that, Foresh took the long view when it came to her pleasure, and it progressed with much cross straddling of yours truly, more than is usually to my pleasure, but it certainly served a dual purpose.

After an interlude wherein the remains of the champagne was quaffed, she pressed her plush lips to mine for the first time, her warm, inviting tongue probing mine playfully. By the dimming light from the windows, her blue eyes sparkled at mine as our lips detached. "You are a good loser, Boone."

"If that's losing, I'll forfeit every time."

"We're going to land soon in Dubai." Her hand found my bishop, whereupon it moved promptly to queen four. "My turn to pleasure you, Boone."

Thus is my abbreviated tale of induction to the Mile High Club, though I cannot say the sky afforded any special advantage or sensation. Well, the landing was certainly memorable. I will never hear the squelch of wheel on tarmac again without thinking of that lusty culmination.

Upon take off from Dubai, we fell asleep, the scent of fresh apples and the touch of her smooth caramel bosom guiding me to slumber.

HAIL LINSENBIGLER!

CHAPTER 7

EMERGING ALONE FROM THE AIRPORT GANGWAY into the terminal was like entering a football stadium from the locker room. Soaring glass ceilings and a second level of shops ringing the walls surrounded me, enormous palm trees and waterfalls in the middle. Yet it was not so much the large space as the large crowd that made it seem like a stadium. The railing on the second level was packed with spectators, and the terminal level was a sea of bobbing heads as far as I could see. All were neatly dressed, men in sport shirts and shorts, women in floral skirts and dresses.

Oddly, my first reaction was that I was underdressed in rumpled shorts, sandals and red hibiscus Hawaiian shirt.

I came to a stop as they all stared at me, their brown faces smiling. This was the first time I would note the prevalence of bright blue eyes among Zarengis, which

57

was quite stunning matched with their lustrous caramel skin.

Is that observation racist? If so, it is on par with my sexism. I prefer the company of women over men.

And then this beautiful multitude cheered – it was New Year's Eve and Times Square all over again as a tumultuous roar erupted from every corner.

Two men and a woman approached. The one leading the pack was black, older, completely bald with round rose lens sunglasses and a cane. He was wearing a white three-piece suit and he was the first to reach me, hand extended.

Mechanically I held out my hand, my eyes still scanning the roiling ocean of cheering spectators.

"Mr. Linsenbigler, I am Watuna, Nambia's mayor." His big leathery hand enveloped mine. He led me forward and waved his silver-handled cane at the crowd. "Welcome to Zarenga Chi!" he boomed.

Thousands of spectators exploded in another round of cheers.

I guessed this welcoming committee explained why I was sent out of the plane last.

Well, almost last. As I stood there stunned by yet more unfounded adulation my eye caught Foresh scooting around me with her roller bag. She shot me a smile, winked and vanished into the crowd.

Two other people were with Watuna – a security detail. The man was a tall black man in dark suit, dark sunglasses and wireless earpiece. The woman was white, with athletic build, short blond hair, and dressed in a dark pant suit and dark sunglasses with a wireless earpiece.

I gave her a double take.

The woman was Tanya.

Yes, that Tanya, the DEA agent from my nightmare entanglement with drug cartels in the Caribbean. I had rescued her from a torture session after which she'd lost her nerve and renounced further undercover work. Subsequently, she had saved me from an axe-wielding maniac in a restaurant. Not the foundation of most relationships, I'll grant you.

And yet the attraction between us prevailed for a brief time as I stayed over the holidays with her in her sailboat in Nassau. Since that time, she had been assigned to DEA training as an instructor at Quantico. Our mutual understanding had been that while we were quite fond of each other, the relationship could never work.

Tanya loves danger; I despise it.

That did not mean I had not harbored tender feelings for her since that time. As you know, I wanted her to come to New York and spend the last week with me there. So this is where she had been reassigned! As part of my security detail!

I blinked at her; she was aloof. This was the second time I had met her while she was working undercover. The first time, of course, I had no idea she was DEA, and she used her obvious womanly charms to vamp me out of getting into trouble. Then she was tanned in a white halter top and short shorts, her violet eyes twinkling mischievously.

The current Zarengi incarnation could hardly have been more different. The black pant suit did not betray much hint of her wild curves and narrow waist. Her manner was not racy and feral, but solemn and blank, those remarkable violet eyes hidden behind reflector sunglasses.

My mind was of course doing backflips.

Clearly she had been sent to Zarenga Chi because of me – this was no coincidence.

If she had been assigned here because of me, that meant some branch of the United States government wanted me to do something other than just be a liquor pitchman for Amalgamated Consumables.

Which in turn meant that I was going to be asked to do something dangerous.

Ice crackled through my veins as I realized my predicament, and without thinking, I turned to go back onto the plane.

Amalgamated can sue me, take all my money, and I would go back to a life of mediocrity, perhaps bartending on some obscure island in the Keys slinging Mia Tais, people pointing and saying: "You know who that is? That bartender used to be Boone Linsenbigler. You don't remember him? He was famous. Then he blew up a fish and nobody ever heard from him again."

Watuna grabbed my arm, laughing, and the audience too roared with laughter, thinking I was joking. He wheeled me around to face the crowd again. "Come, Mr. Linsenbigler!"

With that, the cheering crowd parted as he marched me down the halls of the terminal lined with adoring fans packed cheek by jowl in front of fancy shops, the security detail (including Tanya) right behind us.

Why were all these people cheering? What had I done? Or was it just excitement over having a celebrity in their midst?

At the airport exit was a squad of black men in tan uniforms with assault rifles at the ready.

For future reference and brevity, note that everybody in Zarenga Chi is Zarengi with the wonderful dark skin and blue eyes – unless I note that they are 'white' meaning European. I only make the distinction between races so that the picture of these events is accurately painted.

Emerging from the terminal's envelope of air conditioning, I was assaulted by sunshine and sultry weather. It was every bit of ninety degrees and humid.

On the airport service road ahead was a motorcade: a black limousine with tinted windows bracketed by motorcycle policemen front and back. Beyond them were tall palm trees and lush landscaping, the chevrons of white gulls and black frigate birds sailing across a vibrant blue sky.

Two men in white uniforms and gloves peeled back the doors to the limousine, into the cool confines of which I was promptly seated. Watuna sat next to me, and our security detail sat across and facing us as the doors slammed and the motorcycles around us roared to life.

As our limo glided forward, I averted my eyes from Tanya and onto Watuna, who slapped me on the knee and said: "You have the key to our city!"

"Thank you, that's very generous, Mayor Watuna." I took a deep breath and paused. "Yet I am afraid I don't really understand why your countrymen are so excited to see me, or why I'm getting the key to the city. I was hired by Amalgamated Consumables, and as such I had to become a Zarengi citizen in order to move here for two and a half years. Am I missing something?"

"You are too modest, Mr. Linsenbigler. You are a famous adventurer and American hero. You proved that by earning the Lichtenbichler Cross of Valor by defeating the ZLF terrorist cell in New York."

I thought Noomba said he didn't want news of that to get out? That's why he said I was being whisked away. Unless, of course, that was a lie.

"That was only because the ZLF thought I was a Von Lichtenbichler."

Watuna looked at me blankly. "But you are a Von Lichtenbichler. You are the great, great grandson of Maximillian Von Lichtenbichler. His first wife took their son to America to her uncle in Altoona, Pennsylvania. Her name was changed mistakenly by Irish emigration officials who misunderstood her Bavarian accent."

I sighed, a hand on my forehead. "I don't suppose there's a bar in this limo?"

Watuna smiled and slapped my knee again. "Of course! We know Boone Von Lichtenbichler's love of drink – just like Maximillian." He snapped his fingers at Tanya, who slid open a case on the wall. A silver bar folded out, lit from below, revealing an ice bucket and a glistening row of decanters and tumblers, the barware tinkling one against the other.

Tanya shoveled a few ice cubes in a glass and paused, awaiting my order.

I am of a mind that there are certain moments in life – good and bad – that demand a special drink. After I tangled with a narco-submarine-mounted machine gun, I made myself a depth charge of beer with shot sunk into it. When hiking and camping across the frozen forests of Siberia, I made myself a julep with chewing gum and snow. In a Mongolian desert hut after a day of camel antics and listening to my guide Ghat throat sing, I made a tea-soju sour.

I pointed at the bar. "What's the yellow liquor on the end?"

"Ylang-ylang vodka!" Watuna announced, with obvious but unexplained pride. (By the by, feel free to pronounce that *lang-lang*.)

"Sure, let's have it. And what's the purple stuff?"

"Pineapple port!"

"And a touch of that."

Tanya splashed some of the slightly milky yellow liquid into the glass, then dribbled in the pineapple, which created a snake-like plume, and handed the drink to me. I could only wonder what her eyes might be trying to tell me from behind those sunglasses. Her expression? Expressionless.

I took the glass. "Watuna? Joining me?"

We waved a hand at his feet. "I have the gout."

I know when I'm stuck, and there was no use struggling to escape at that juncture. My fate was sealed as soon as I stepped off the gangway. No sense not having a cocktail as your ship slowly slips beneath the waves.

So I raised my glass. "Ganbei!" *Cheers* in Chinese, and I reflected briefly on the last time I said that. Place: Mountains of Eastern Kazakhstan, in an isolated hunting cabin next to a small trout stream in a narrow canyon. Company: the lovely but moody Lotus. Cocktail: makeshift mint juleps by the fire. The Mood: tense. We tried not to let on, but we each knew the next day might be our last. That was the night before one of the most arduous and dangerous days of my life.

Reflecting on that in the back of that cool limousine helped me remain calm. I didn't think the next day would be bad. Though because of my situation in Zarenga Chi, my instincts told me another 'predicament' was approaching just as sure as the next cocktail hour.

I sipped, my eyes scanning the tropical paradise outside: swaying palms, eruptions of flowers, lawns, and bright white stucco buildings, all backed in the near distance by a turquoise ocean, mountains rising into the sky ahead in the distance. Everywhere there seemed to be people tending to the lush plants.

As we rounded a bend in the road, a much taller mountain appeared, a black forbidding silhouette with smoke rising lazily from the peak. I gestured with my drink: "That's the volcano?"

Watumba nodded gravely. "That is Mumu, a sacred place."

"Does it ever erupt?"

"Mumu rumbles and smokes, but she does not explode. We are told by geologists that because Mumu continues to release pressure, she will not explode. Yet, after both Maximillian von Lichtenbichler and his son died, both times, Mumu shook the island violently."

"Are those hot air balloons up there?"

"Indeed so. Zarengis are avid balloonists."

At once flowery and honeyed, the cocktail made me think of bananas and lychee nuts. The hint of pineapple's malic acidity helped balance the floral notes and avert perfumasceousness. Most importantly, though, the libation was strong. "So where are we headed, Watuna?"

"Your testimonial dinner!"

I tugged at my red hibiscus shirt. "Don't you think I'm a little under-dressed?'

He smiled knowingly, and by the light of the window his blue eyes twinkled behind the rose sunglasses. "We have made arrangements for an interlude in which you will be properly attired."

"So is my employer going to be at this dinner?"

"Certainly. Dermot Kinkaid is on the King's Council, and he will be there."

"He's Amalgamated's CEO, right?"

"Indeed."

CHAPTER 8

BELIEVE IT OR NOT, in my week kicking around the most rarified bars in Manhattan, I had not only researched Indian Ocean angling but how Zarenga Chi came to its current state of high living.

The north coast of ZC had a natural deep water bay. In the 1970's, the kingdom struck a deal with Titan Transport to build a container port that would not only service Titan's international shipping interests but also provide facilities to bring goods to the kingdom. Titan was given free hand to run all shipping concessions as long as they agreed to maintain and operate the port and kept the channels dredged. By extension, Titan became ZC's *de facto* Commerce Department.

This deal brought large engineering and construction firms to the island to design the ports, and to provide dredging and install piers. These same firms were offered a tax-free haven in exchange for building new infrastructure.

These arrangements snowballled.

Sealife Harvesting moved in and leased a port for their fishing fleets, and became the nation's seafood supplier. International Aggregate arrived to ship materials for concrete to the Middle East from Australia and became the Department of Transportation. LGB Coastal needed a home base while installing a nearby undersea conduits, and ZC cut a deal whereby LGB revamped the capital's telephone cable system.

More companies came, as did more free and complex infrastructure, to include new water mains, electrical lines and natural gas systems. TransPetro attained exclusive rights to sell fuel on the islands, and provided geothermal wells into the volcanic substrata. Water Reclamation International, servicing the Middle East's water demands, became the nation's water supply and sewage treatment department.

The central bank and de facto treasury was even privatized and transformed the kingdom into an offshore bank and money haven.

Amalagmated Consumables, my employer, became the sole provider of imported beverages and food, and became responsible for the safety and quality of the food supply.

So in effect, Zarenga Chi had outsourced the entire government in return for improvements to their infrastructure and in exchange for monopolies and tax-free status.

As a result, the monarchy became increasingly beholden to the corporations, who attained permanemt seats on the King's Council. What was good for the corporations was seen as good for the kingdom.

And what was good for the native Zarengi? They obtained a cushy safety net in exchange for becoming a servant class, which in turn spawned the Zarengi Liberation Front who took exception to this arranegment.

It was with this history in mind that I found myself in a white dinner jacket/tuxedo before an audience of the corporate elite. They were almost entirely European or Asian. Likely, they were all Zarengi citizens – the imported kind like myself.

The audience at the airport was almost entirely black.

So my testimonial was being thrown by the upper echelon. Nothing wrong with that, I suppose. Rich people run things and always have. As an American, though, I'm obviously troubled when this divide is also a racial one. True, Watuna was sitting at the dais to my left, and he looked as if he was doing well enough. But he was the only native Zarengi in the room other than the waiters, waitresses and busboys.

My red Cross of Valor was hung around my neck, centered on my breastplate. My hair had been slicked back on the sides. A barber had shaved me, leaving me with V-whiskers below my lip. Above my lip, my mustache was beginning to reclaim its former glory. Before me was a plush, crowded ballroom brimming with elites dressed to the nines and sitting in rapt attention as to what my comments would be. Behind them was an enormous glass wall looking out over a rocky coastline, frothy with waves and blue seas.

As Master Cocktailer, I had gained some proficiency in making public appearances and speaking off the cuff, so addressing audiences came relatively easy to me, and I was able to formulate what to say and how to say it with élan. Being a tad liquored up never hurt either, except perhaps that I was a little more willing to express what was on my mind.

"Ladies and gentlemen and fellow Zarengis, I cannot express how humbled I am by the honor that has been bestowed upon me with this Cross of Valor. Likewise, I cannot adequately express how undeserving I feel. My abduction by the ZLF in New York was a situation that simply befell me, and I credit the close cooperation between my native country and Zarenga Chi for their interdiction and capture of that terrorist cell. As such, because I did not in fact do anything to earn this cross, I cannot in good conscience accept this honor for myself."

There was a hushed gasp.

"I will, however, accept it for the everyday Zarengi, those who turned out to the airport to welcome me. I would like it enshrined there so all who land on our shores can witness this tribute to the guiding spirit of this kingdom. It is the native Zarengi who are the enduring patriots of this country, who through their hard work, perseverance and dedication make this kingdom a shining example of literacy and high living standards." I picked up my ylang-ylang martini and raised it. "A toast!"

The audience got to their feet, and raised their glasses.

"To everyday Zarengi!" I bellowed.

Hazzah! They roared, erupting into mad applause.

I looked down the dais at Watuna, and he was practically in tears, nodding and clapping furiously.

I looked to my right, from whence Dermot Kinkaid stood and sidled up next to me. I had met him only briefly prior to the dinner, and merely exchanged pleasantries. He was early sixties, with a ruddy complexion and thick features as if he had toiled in harsh weather, though I doubted he had. Dermot was so craggy that he looked carved from rock. Yet he donned glasses with blond rims, and wore his hair in a crew cut, greying blond hair standing straight up off his big skull. Bemused eyes with long lashes sat above a cobble-sized nose and wide, perpetual grin. He placed one large hand on my shoulder, and used the other to pump my hand. He edged me aside and leaned into the microphone, straightening his bowtie.

"Ladies and gentlemen, I think I speak for all of us when I say that Boone Linsenbigler, like his bitters, is a tonic for this nation." His gravelly voice had a Scottish lilt. My name from his lips came out more like *beun* than *boon*.

"Boone's words perfectly express what I personally believe to be true, and what every Zarengi should also hold dear. Yes, we are a wealthy nation, and our society is stratified just as any other. But we, above many others

71

including the richest nations on earth to include the United States, feel we are duty-bound to provide for all our citizens; that it is morally essential for those of us with more to help and nurture those with less. So it is heartening to hear that Boone, a new citizen and great grandson of Maximillian von Lichtenbichler, is in every sense of the word, a Zarengi patriot."

The crowd was on its feet again, cheering and clapping, and everybody looking at me with the glow of patriotic pride.

I waved my glass again, my smile wavering slightly as I realized that I had inadvertently made a political speech when I was just trying to be humble and ease my discomfort at schilling for the corporate masters.

I had not anticipated the Zarengi establishment's self-consciousness in that same regard. Likely the Zarengi Liberation Front had compelled them to worry about this and the stability of the nation they had built. So here I come along and let them off the hook while at the same time placating the underclass by putting my Cross of Valor in a display case at the airport. What I had done, when you think about it, is precisely what a good politician does: convinces the common man that he's helping them when he's actually helping his campaign donors and stuffing his pockets. A dirty business to be sure, which is why I so resolutely disdain any involvement in politics. Or taking sides.

Alas, this was Times Square all over again, where I'd been put on stage by elected officials and lauded by the

Governor. A Senator had leaned in to me and asked "What are your affiliations, son?"

I thwarted his and the governor's attempt to politicize me.

Now I'd just blundered blindly, or perhaps tipsily, into a political tiger trap.

I took a deep breath, scanning the adoring crowd, thinking: *All right, Boonie, don't panic, nobody has asked you to do anything or participate yet, you can always say no. Besides, Zarenga Chi is a monarchy, there are no elected officials, and the King's Council is comprised of appointees, and wouldn't need a novice like me trying to advise the king.*

A number of other luminaries made speeches similar to Dermot's, and even after the meal was over and the crowd began to disperse, I had to endure another hour of handshakes until I caught the attention of Dermot as he passed near.

"Mr. Kinkaid, would it be rude of me to ask that I might retire for the evening? I've traveled a long way and admit to feeling the effects of jetlag."

Without batting his long lashes he snapped his fingers at my security detail standing nearby and waved them over. "Take Boone to his apartment." He patted me on the shoulder. "Again, perfect speech, Linsenbigler. You and I will meet tomorrow and discuss your future."

I didn't like the sound of that.

CHAPTER 9

BRIGHT SUNSHINE AND LAUGHING GULLS woke me the next morning. I sat up in a king-sized bed with white sateen sheets and too many pillows. Filmy curtains at the window undulated with a salty sea breeze.

On the railing of a balcony sat a big fat gull guffawing at the top of his avian lungs. I tossed a pillow at the open window, and when it hit the curtains the bird took flight and relative quietude was restored.

I took a deep breath and tried to recall the close of the previous day.

My memory was compromised not so much by all the ylang-ylang martinis as by succumbing to slumber in the back of the limousine piloted by Tanya and her fellow security guard. I recalled being roused and cajoled to the door of a harborside townhouse where two other security people stood sentry. The one security detail handed me off to the two black gentlemen at the abode, which meant Tanya was off duty, somewhere. When was she going to come clue me in to what diabolical task lay before me?

My memory faded after stumbling in the door – knowing me, I found the first available bed and dove in. Frankly, I was surprised I had not awoken on the couch or in a Barcalounger.

Through my fingers I surveyed the bedroom – all white and impossibly bright.

The side tables and vanity with mirror were white.

The dresser and wardrobe were white.

The open door to the bathroom revealed that it too, was all white.

I mused that this overly-white scene was like that on a cloud, like the Pearly Gates and Heaven, though I further mused that my final destination might be less white and more brimstone.

Not white at all was the jagged pile of bags, duffels and rod tubes in the corner of the room. These constituted my earthly belongings.

I staggered from bed, and fell upon my boat bag, the one with the essentials for fishing the open sea. In a side pocket I found my sunglasses and slid them on my face with a gasp of relief. From another bag, I donned shorts and sandals, remaining shirtless.

Plodding from the bedroom into the hallway, I was dressed only in my shorts.

The floors were tropical hardwood strewn with colorful tribal rugs. The rooms to either side looked like a den and a spare bedroom. Before me were curving stairs that took me down to the living room level. Probably sixty feet wide by sixty feet deep, the room's end was all sliding glass doors with a full-width deck over the water. Beyond were other modern townhouses and moored sailboats across the bay. I suppose by 'modern' I mean the architecture was rectilinear Prairie Style, like Frank Lloyd Wright, sleek with lots of glass.

Carved from the near end of the living room was an open kitchenette and bar lined with tribal print bar stools. The place was airy and segmented by rattan and wicker furniture.

On the bar was an enormous fruit basket.

I found coffee, filters and the coffee maker, and deftly put them to the task of providing the essential morning elixir.

Plucking what looked like a small peach from the fruit basket, I went to the window next to the front door, peering through the gauzy curtains to the street. My townhouse was in a landscaped development of some kind, the dwellings not crammed together but lazily spaced with dockage and open bulkhead in between. Palms, bougainvillea and palmettoes dotted the lawns. Parked in front of my unit was a black limousine with the two male security guards in black suits and sunglasses in the front seat. One studied his phone while the other gazed into the distance.

I bit into my peach and found that it was something like a peach but with a more citrusy red flesh that was slightly bitter. Not bad – certainly worthy of a vodka or rum infusion.

There was yet another staircase down from the living room, and I descended into an enclosed dock area where a nice little white skiff bobbed in the clear aquamarine water, schools of striped baitfish darting under the dock. I hadn't realized it, but my townhouse was not just on the harbor, it was over it. My townhouse was in effect a boathouse, with a marine garage space under the living room. My finger jabbed a button on the wall and the garage door opened, sunlight and sea air pouring in.

Well, this was a spiffy arrangement, aye? *Me like!*

Hopping into the boat, I turned the ignition key and the dash lit up. It had a full tank, and when I thumbed the choke and gave her a crank, the silver Honda 90 outboard sputtered to life, purring and ready to go.

My impulse was to dash upstairs, grab my gear and a shirt, and go for a little ride to see if I could score a few finny friends.

That's when I heard a doorbell, presumably mine.

I switched the boat off and ascended the stair to the front door landing.

Please let this be someone delivering breakfast.

A look through the curtain revealed that there was yet another Rolls-Royce black limo in front of my townhouse, behind the one containing my security detail, this one with a crest painted on the side – two crossed palm trees with a crown inset. Likewise, the front fenders had pennants with the same symbol flapping lazily in the breeze.

The doorbell sounded again, so I shrugged and opened the door, forgetting that I was just in my shorts.

Two large Zarengi quickly filled the doorway – both were large and strong enough to have played center in the NFL. They were packed into black suits and they dispensed with any formalities by coming directly toward me. I backpedaled into the living room as more giant men in dark suits filed in behind them, each with stern looks and darting eyes. Curling around the breakfast bar I found refuge on a stool at the end, my living room filling with what were obviously more security people. Some looked behind the curtains while others checked a hall closet and another trotted upstairs.

The brute nearest me pointed a large dark finger at my face: "Are you the only one here?" His voice was loud and accusatory.

It took me a moment to find my voice: "Y-Yes."

One man came up from the boat bay and another down from upstairs and announced "Clear!"

Brute still looked unhappy, but looked away from me and said into his wrist: "All clear."

The squad of giant black men in suits stationed themselves in the four corners of the room and at all the entrances as Brute positioned himself behind a large wicker chair. Two more came in the door and stood on either side of the open door. I'm not sure, but I think there were ten in all by this point.

An entirely different kind of man was next to enter. He was in a pristine white track suit and white loafers.

Plump and soft looking, he was a light-skinned black man with full features and a pug nose. He had wide feminine blue eyes and a close-cropped Afro that looked dyed to me. Two final goons trailed behind him.

As he rounded the bar he raised his chin and looked down his pug nose at me. But he kept moving until he reached the wicker chair with Brute standing behind it. With what looked like a pirouette, he spun and sat in the chair, slowly crossing his legs and folding his hands over one knee, one white loafer waving. His manner was impatient.

"Can someone get Linsenbigler a shirt?" His voice was shrill. I heard someone dash upstairs.

What the devil is this?

I can only imagine what my expression was at the time. I admit that my surprise was dissolving into dismay and heading toward my own impatient manner.

Can't people just leave me alone? Must I be prevailed upon at every turn?

I found my voice, and for some reason I chose to say: "Would you like some coffee?" I could smell that it was ready, and I was ready. *"Who the hell are you?"* might have passed my lips, but one doesn't get snippy with anybody trailing a troop of twelve bodyguards.

His eyes narrowed at me. "Do you know who I am?"

Looking around the room, and reflecting on the Rolls-Royce flying the royal seal, I cleared my throat and said: "His Majesty, Maximillian III?"

The thinnest of grins tugged at his full lips. "Someone get us coffee," he hissed.

A goon appeared with my blue fishing shirt and handed it to me, while I heard another in the kitchen opening cabinets.

As I buttoned my shirt, I asked: "Your Highness, to what do I owe this unexpected pleasure?"

"You know damn well why I'm here. They mean to replace me with you." He rolled his eyes petulantly away from me and out the glass doors. "I won't permit it. I will not abdicate. So you might as well go home."

"In all candor, Your Highness, I have no intention of allowing anybody to make me king of Zarenga Chi." I accepted a mug of coffee from a goon, who delivered one to Maximillian, and whispered: "Four sugars."

Max nodded at him, and as the minion retreated, His Highness sipped his sugary coffee, smacking his chubby lips. He turned his eyes back to me. "There is much you do not understand, Linsenbigler. Did you ever wonder why they would want to make you king in place of me?"

I sipped my own coffee and shrugged. "I've wondered, all right. Though I'm becoming accustomed to not knowing why or what people want me to do until it's too late to extricate myself from their little plans. My problem is that I have a contractual obligation to Amalgamated Consumables. They own me. If they say I stay here, I have to, at least for two plus years until my contract expires."

"Even at the cost of your life?" he growled.

I raised an eyebrow. "Why would they want to make me king and then kill me?"

He smirked. "There are only you and I left as heirs to the Lichtenbichler throne. Once the dynasty ends, it will be the final blow, this will no longer be a kingdom, even if it is now mostly a kingdom in name only."

"If you die and I refuse to take the throne then it amounts to the same thing. And believe me, I will refuse the throne, and nobody can force me to take it."

Max slurped his coffee, and enjoyed a short chuckle. "Perhaps. Their problem is that the Codicils of the Realm do not clearly specify what happens if there are no more heirs to the throne or who is in charge if the last king dies. Of course, they assume that the King's Council will take command, but they would still need to institute some sort of leader, and you can be assured that they would not hold open elections to do so. What they want is to make this an oligarchy with authoritarian control. Why? Because that's the corporate culture they know. They want to put the final touches of turning this nation into a corporation."

"So why would they want me?"

"Status quo. They think you will be compliant. I, on the other hand, have been pushing back, and have been trying to negotiate with them to turn this country into a constitutional monarchy as it should be, with elections and representation."

I winced. "So how's that going?"

"It's not. As King, the codicils do give me the power to institute a change of government unilaterally. Why, you ask, don't I do so?"

I merely shrugged.

"Because the King's Council might push back or use the military in a power struggle. And because I have the ability to reign in the King's Council with this thumb drive, encased in titanium, hermetically sealed." He opened his shirt to reveal a silver capsule about the size of the end of a thumb. It was on a chain around his neck, and with his fingers he gave it a little shake so I could hear the contents rattle. "I can bring this whole corporate monstrosity to its knees unless they make reforms. They know this now, and so should you. The ZLF is right, this has all gone too far."

I shook my head. "But why then did the ZLF kidnap me? You – and by extension I – have the power to bring reforms."

He snorted. "They were lured into doing so by your secret agencies and the FBI, told that you were coming to replace me as a corporate shill. Why? Because your government is in lock step with mine to maintain the status quo, keep business humming, and perhaps to look out for the interests of friends in high places. By having the ZLF kidnap you, and then rescuing you, the agencies made you look like a hero and demonized the ZLF in the eyes of the populace. You got a hero's welcome at the airport and my subjects are primed for you to succeed me. And yet, do you realize they have instituted exit visas? The people cannot leave the country without permission. They are prisoners, just like I am. And you. As a Zarengi citizen, you, too, need an exit visa. For me, this is the last straw. With the information on this thumb drive I can expose those friends in high places, expose the use of our treasury as their piggy bank, unless they begin the process of reform."

I nodded at the silver capsule. "I don't know what that capsule is and I don't want to know. But if the information on that thumb drive has the power that you say it does, you'd better watch your step, Your Majesty."

He swept his hand at the goons. "I still have the Imperial Guard. They are armed to the teeth. My limo is bulletproof and bombproof. I'm watching my step." With a groan he set his coffee mug aside and shoved his way out of the chair and onto his white loafers. "I'm pleased we had this little chat and understand each other."

"I am as well. Ascending to the throne of Zarenga Chi is the last thing I would ever do."

Max twisted his plump lips into a sharp smile. "It might indeed be the last thing you would ever do." He snapped his fingers and the goons hustled toward the door. Once outside, they formed a gauntlet leading out to the Rolls-Royces. Two goons in tow, His Majesty Maximillian Lichtenbichler III trundled out the front door, leaving it open.

My security detail stood outside their limo, and they bowed their heads as the king approached.

I leaned on the doorframe, watching Max disappear into the limo, four goons after him, and the other goons piled into the other limo. Shaking my head, I worried about that plump little man. What if they did kill him? The crosshairs would be directly on me to ascend to the throne. The very thought sent a shiver through my sternum.

The Rolls-Royces started to drive away.

They detonated simultaneously.

The blast was like a clap of thunder, like lightening splintering a mighty pine or cracking a granite mountain peak.

The shock wave knocked me off my feet, which was a good thing because flying glass and shards of metal flew over me.

My townhouse shook so violently that I thought the place would collapse.

Rolling to my side and onto my feet, my eyes beheld the two limos roiled in flame, black smoke billowing into the pristine blue tropical skies.

My security detail scrambled up from where they had been knocked down, and steadied themselves on their limo. They wagged their heads like a couple of drunks trying to sober up.

I dashed down toward the flaming wrecks not knowing why. At first thought I might be able to help somebody, but it was clear there was no surviving such an explosion. The cars may have been bomb proof from the outside, but clearly not from the inside. The roofs were splayed open like blossoming black flowers.

Through the ringing in my ears, I heard a boat motor start.

I looked toward the bulkhead at the side of my townhouse.

A blue paneled speedboat pulled away from the sea wall.

In it were four black beatniks in sunglasses, fists held high.

It didn't take advanced calculus to figure out that they had been the ones to detonate the bombs.

Idiots! He was on your side!

Anger seized my brain, a cauldron of outrage and resentment. Yes, resentment at having been once more dragged into a situation where I felt helpless and in grave danger.

Max was dead.

Long Live his Majesty Boone the First!

My legs pumped as I raced back into my abode and down the stairs. I tossed the ropes to the boat and hopped in, my vision blurred by rage. I cranked the Mercury and slammed her into reverse, spinning the wheel, and ramming the boat into drive.

What on earth I was doing, you may well ask? We're familiar with my distaste for danger or risking my life for any reason. Unlike the persona advertised on TV for the sale of cocktail amenities, I am not a 'man of action.' I am compelled to act as a matter of desperation and to escape peril.

After my trials in Russia, I had been left feeling grievously manipulated to the extent that I felt violated. And then to be sold to Amalgamated and not have any recourse…and then to be kidnapped and shot through the ear…

Outwardly, I seem to have accepted these episodes with calm and resignation as if I am somehow fated to these turns of events. I'm ever hopeful that each ill fortune will be the last, fingers crossed that if I can just stick it out, the skies will clear, and people will stop trying to put me in harm's way.

But it just keeps coming.

Yet there's a psychological toll, a resentment that builds from persistent manipulation. There's a limit to how much you can tolerate before you snap.

Inaction, hoping, dodging: those weren't going to make it stop.

I needed to take control; I needed to chase down these assassins.

And not just because they murdered thirteen people.

My fury was that they had done so to manipulate me into becoming King.

I wasn't going to let them get away with it, not this time.

The line was drawn.

I'm not taking it anymore.

CHAPTER 10

MY SKIFF WAS ON PLANE IN SECONDS, my hair raked by the salt air and my shirttails flapping. I had the beatnik boat in my crosshairs. It was about eight hundred feet ahead, but I was closing.

It was about then that one of them looked back my way and pointed. Then they all looked back, the man at the helm jamming the throttle all the way forward.

Sleek white townhouses and languorous-looking palm trees streamed by on both sides as I snaked my way in the wake of the boat ahead of me. I was no longer gaining on them, merely holding my distance.

Ahead was a low causeway – high enough for our boats but not for any masted vessels. Beyond I could see another bay surrounded by apartment buildings, small sailboats tacking here and there in the light breeze.

What would I do if I caught up with them? There were four of them and one of me. I resolved mostly to follow them and see where they went. With any luck run I hoped to pass a police boat.

Of course, I was only in sunglasses, blue fishing shirt, shorts, and sandals, devoid of any cell phone.

Ah, but the boat had a marine radio. I know from fishing trips far and wide that Channel 16 is the international distress channel, so I flicked on the set and dialed in that frequency.

"Mayday, mayday, mayday."

I released the call button and reflexively ducked as I zoomed under the concrete and steel causeway, bursting out the other side into a wider bay. The boat steered in a wide curve to the right, toward a canal flanked on both sides by light blue apartment buildings.

A woman's voice came over the speaker. She had a lilt to her voice and sounded for all the world like Foresh. To think only a day ago I was safely ensconced with that lovely girl in a happy state of Denge Chippo sex hangover. *Now this!*

"This is Zarenga Chi Constabulary. State your emergency. Over."

"King Max was just assassinated and I am in a boat following his killers." I released the button, wiping salt spray from my sunglasses with the back of my sleeve.

The radio just crackled, static, for probably fifteen seconds as I darted my skiff around a sailboat. Then a man's earnest voice came on – just as the boat ahead was entering the canal and past the "NO WAKE" signs.

"Your location, please."

"I don't know where I am, this is only my second day in Zarenga Chi."

"Can you describe your surroundings? Over."

The blue apartment buildings passed on either side. "Entering a canal from a bay and there are light blue apartment buildings on both sides. By the sun to my right, I'd say I'm heading north. Over."

"What does their boat look like? Over."

"Four black men in dark sunglasses and black berets. And white short-sleeve shirts. Their boat is white with blue panels. I'm approximately a hundred yards back from them in an all-white skiff, and I have a blue shirt. Over."

"Stay with them. We know where you are and will intercept as soon as we can. Keep the radio on to this frequency. Over."

Boats parked at docks on both sides lunged and bucked from the waves of the beatnik boat, the stray people up on the bulkheads waving their hands in the air to get us to slow down. Coming at us, a citizen came slowly toward us in a speed boat, and he too waved at us to slow down, but we roared past his angry shouts drowned out by the motor roar. Pastel bungalows and palms streamed by on either side.

We came around a corner and a low drawbridge was slowly coming down, red lights flashing, cars waiting on either side. Even the approaches to the bridge had nicely manicured sloping embankments and flower beds.

As we approached, I realized the bridge would likely be too low by the time I reached it for me to pass under.

Not so the beatniks, who all crouched in anticipation of narrowly passing under the descending bridge.

I reflected on how the boats in Baja Sur land on the beach each day. The guides run their boats full speed up onto the beach. One would think that the propeller would be destroyed by this maneuver. However, if you unlock the motor tilt and trim it up all the way, the beach hits the skeg at the bottom of the motor and forces it into the up position. The propeller never comes in contact with the sand.

The flower beds and lawns on the sides of the bridge were no steeper than the beach at in Baja. The worst that could happen? My boat would land on the roadway, the hull torn to shreds.

I reached back and unlocked the motor tilt.

The beatniks slid under the bridge and the halves of the structure came together and stopped about three feet above the water.

I swerved, aiming for the flower beds.

Thumbing the trim lever, I raised the propeller to just under the water, which slowed me just a little.

The safety barriers holding the traffic back on either side began to rise.

Crouching, knees bent, I prepared for the worst. Ah, well, I really didn't want to catch them anyway, did I? I'd radioed the police, and done my part and then some. What lunatic would have given chase, and in doing so, tried this ridiculous stunt?

At the last second, the flower beds close at hand, I realized that the guides in Baja also killed the motor at the last second.

Hand turning the key, I felt a jolt, then the vibration of the hull slicing up the embankment.

Nothing came next. That is, there was no vibration. There was just the wind through my hair and whiskers.

I would imagine the motorists were more than a little surprised by the sight of my boat launching across the road. Likely I was no more than a foot or two over the road, an explosion of mulch and flower petals in my wake as I was launched through the air.

Gripping the wheel, I blinked blurry-eyed at the blue water on the opposite side, impact imminent.

Hull slamming onto the water, I flexed my knees and kept my balance, remaining in a crouch.

The motor fell back into the down position.

I cranked the motor back to life and thumbed the trim to re-submerge the propeller to optimal depth.

Throttle: thrust forward.

If there is such a thing as luck, I'd just used it all.

The canal stretched ahead, an open bay beyond. The beatniks were now further out ahead.

The expressions of the beatniks when they looked back and saw me still in their wake was priceless: confounded disbelief, like men witnessing an apparition or sea monster.

Seen a ghost, have you? Ha! You'll have to do better than that to escape Linsenbigler!

BRIAN M. WIPRUD

My flippant thoughts were more to reassure myself than actual bravado. I regretted having succeeded in getting past that bridge. After all, who would have blamed me for simply stopping and giving up? The police would likely catch the beatniks in any case.

Curving starboard into the bay, the view was not of apartments or condos, but of large ships. I could see a container port in the distance. Piers within the first mile on the right jutted far out into the bay, and they were chockablock with undersea cabling ships, tugs, buoy tenders, and fishing trawlers.

Piers on the left were parked with Russian naval ships exclusively, and there was a security boom and buoys that prevented any approach by water.

Flashing blue lights of police cars appeared on a road further right that traced the shoreline. Huzzah! The cavalry! Though I would have preferred the navy.

The beatniks were likely another football field out from me, and heading for where the ships were parked. Specifically, for the largest cabling ships.

Cabling ships have all manner of high, trussed-steel armatures for feeding cable over the stern and into the sea. To me, all the arched yellow arms made it look like a roller coaster was aboard the ship. While avoiding violent television shows, I once saw a documentary on how these ships lay thousands of miles of cable across the ocean. That's the only reason I recognized the ship for what it was.

The beatniks were full speed ahead toward the back of the boat and the bulkhead. Did they intend to climb ashore there? If so, I hoped the constables arrived in time to nab them. Or did they intend to slip through and around the other side, a maneuver designed simply to slow me down in their wake?

As it drew close, the boat slowed. It vanished behind the ship – between it and the bulkhead.

I arrived at the spot where they vanished a minute or so later, slowed and craned my neck to see where they had gone. There was only twenty feet between the back of the moored ship and the steel sheeting of the bulkhead, but there was no boat, so I inched my way into the space, toward the corner. Could I have been wrong about them motoring into the spot?

When I reached the far side of the ship, I looked around the corner of the hull. Above, large white mooring bolsters wedged the ship's hull about eight feet from the bulkhead. About halfway, in that tight spot, I saw the beatnik boat. They were still in it, but they were arguing, their motor growling and churning.

My guess was that the ship had moved slightly and pinched them in there. Their original motives for going this direction would never be known to me.

Was I wrong, or were they arguing in Russian? I know phrases, and having lived in New York and New Jersey, was very familiar with the sound of the language even if I could not make out the exact words.

The kicker was that when they saw me, the arguing ended, and one of them clearly said *pizdyets*. Decorum prohibits me from explaining exactly what that means, though the gist of it in this context is *we're done*.

The rail of the ship was not that high, and they were quick to abandon the boat and begin hoisting each other up.

There was nobody to hoist me up, but there were some handholds and roller brackets so that I could climb up onto a platform just below the deck.

Killing the motor, I dropped anchor and tossed out my own rubber bolsters. You might think in the moment that I was so focused on the beatniks and righting wrong, but always at the back of my mind is fishing and I didn't want to lose that skiff. This insanity would likely be over soon enough and then I could turn my attention to more important pursuits like wahoo and sailfish.

The climb was not as easy as I thought mostly because the surfaces I was trying to cling to had a thin film of oil and sea salt on them. But I was clawing over the white railing in under a minute. The way the ship is configured, there was not a clear path along the starboard side to where the beatniks were coming aboard, but I poked my head over the side and saw that they were having trouble hoisting up the last man. The straggler had just gotten hold of the railing, but when his comrades saw me, they cursed: "*Blyat!*" Summarily, the three on deck abandoned their companion and winked off somewhere, leaving the straggler literally hanging. Left to fend for himself, the straggler cursed: "*Otvali, mudak, blyat!*"

I only recognized the words for *asshole* and *fuck*.

Next to me was a ladder up to the next level, and I climbed it, then made my way forward between the yellow roller coaster armatures, around a large curved cable bin to where it met the tall part of the ship. There was a ladder down – I looked to see the straggler with his arms over the railing trying to raise his feet between the railings so he could climb aboard. His frustration had got the better of him, and he was fairly blubbering over his predicament.

Close enough to see this beatnik more closely, it became clear that this was not a beatnik of the same pedigree as those who had abducted me in New York.

The straggler was wearing brown grease paint on his face.

He was in blackface, and likely it was one of his arms that during the struggle to clamber on deck had wiped a swath of black complexion to reveal a white complexion.

Russians.

Max was right, there was a lot going on here that I didn't understand.

This turn of events actually worked in my favor – I could subdue one man but not all four. And this one was shorter and more slender than I.

I looked for a weapon in my immediate vicinity. The only object at hand was hanging on a hook next to a winch: a torque wrench. It was the length of my forearm to my fingertips with a socket head at the end.

As I climbed down the ladder, Straggler had clambered between the railings and was wriggling onto the deck.

As he got to his feet, eyes wild and mouth panting, I confronted him, wrench in hand.

I expected some calculus on his part, and a pause as he considered what his next move should be.

I expected incorrectly.

Launching forward, he bowled into me amidships before I could swing the wrench. Off balance I stumbled and fell to my side as he tumbled but rolled onto his feet on the other side of me.

He was off like a shot.

I dashed after him.

He'd gotten sufficient lead to find the gangway to the pier, but stopped abruptly at the sight of the tiny constable cars whirring down the pier toward us, little blue lights blinking.

Straggler thought better of his escape toward the pier and police, turning away from the gangway and dashing up a staircase toward the bridge.

Following, I lost sight of him, and so began peering in windows and doors – he might lie in wait and try to sandbag me. So I lost time by slowly peering around corners.

Perhaps he had decided to hide? Likely there were many places for that on a ship with so many complicated cable wielding machines.

When I reached the aft railing of the foredeck, I spied him clambering up one of the yellow roller coaster gantries.

My first reaction was puzzlement. Clambering up there was like a fox escaping hounds by climbing a tree: he would be cornered. My eye traced the gantry up to where the far end of it – perhaps seventy feet off the aft deck – curved over the stern. At the end of it was a winch cable down. A hook at the end of it was hanging just over the aft deck near my boat.

Down below me was an immense round turret for feeding cable up the armatures. I could see no way down to the top of it from where I was standing. Even if I found a way, there was all manner of rollers and machinery blocking egress to the aft part of the ship.

So there was no path fast enough to the stern on deck to head off Straggler.

Except up the armature. Yet that would put Straggler seventy feet up. Once he reached the end, where to?

Ah! He aimed to slide down that cable.

He was headed to my boat!

He was too far along the armature for me to have any hopes of scrambling up there after him.

My father was a man of many dubious quotes that meant nothing but were concocted to sound as if they did. These utterances came to mind at odd moments. I would picture him standing over me as a lad, his thin hair slicked back, his heavy-browed specs making his eyes overly large. He was fond of tweed vests and bow ties. The thumb of one hand hooked in his vest pocket, the other hand's fingers pointing the stem of his pipe at me, I could picture him nodding wisely. The only nugget of his wisdom that came to me in that moment was: *When the soup catches fire, eat steak.*

I suppose you could say in that instance the soup was indeed on fire, and I was all for steak, all for another option.

My eyes traced the cable that ran through the armature gantry down to where it vanished into a portal three feet below me. The cable was over an inch thick. If I jumped on it I doubt that I could have moved it enough to make it more than pulse all the way up at the end of the armature. On one side of me on the wall was a fire cabinet with a hose and axe. No, the axe would have been pathetic and no match for a steel cable of that thickness. To the other side, the wall was just port holes, a door, and then another cabinet. I trotted over to take a look: *Emergency Cable Saw.*

I blinked at the words. What? Why would such a thing...

I recalled from the documentary that when undersea cables were being laid, they were understandably under huge amounts of stress. If the cable twisted when it came off the spool and jammed in the armature mayhem would ensue. Because the ship cannot come to an instant stop, a snag in the cable can be disastrous – the armature would twist and splinter, shards of metal shooting out into anyone standing by. The broken truss might rake across the deck sweeping the crew into the ocean in a mangled heap. If the cable snapped, it might whip across the deck and further lay waste to those on hand.

The saw was designed to cut the huge cables in just such an emergency.

It looked like a chain saw, yet it had no teeth, just a diamond-encrusted disc. A hose was attached to it, and a turn of a spigot in the cabinet brought water that hissed and dripped from the saw. The hose rolled off a drum and I pulled it over to where the winch cable was.

Like most chainsaws, this one was cantankerous and did not want to get out of bed, as it were. I pulled, it puttered, and I played with the choke…

Glancing up, I could see Straggler had reached the end of the armature.

I heard excited voices and footsteps on the gangway – the police. Yet they were not in any better position to stop Straggler than I. Shoot him down? The constables in Zarenga Chi, as in some other rarified countries, do not carry firearms, only batons.

All at once the saw came to life, though I had to feather the choke to keep her from stalling.

Straggler was about five feet into his descent down the cable when the saw's blade – water flying from the cowling – sliced though that inch thick cable like a hot knife through cream cheese.

The cable parted.

But the ends just curled.

That damned cable just sat there and didn't move.

I thumbed off the saw and groaned, looking to the sky for some divine guidance. *Why, Lord, hand me the saw if this was the result?*

Grinding, the cut cable began to slowly move up the armature.

This was even worse, an insult to injury. This was actually helping straggler descend faster!

All at once, there was a deafening crack as the cable shot pell-mell up through the armature, the end banging against the struts like a drum roll as it went.

When the end of the cable shot out of the high end of the armature gantry, it cracked like a whip.

Straggler was almost on the aft deck and so jumped the last five feet.

Yet the force of the cable spinning out through the top of the gantry whirled the cable next to him, and looped around his midsection.

The body of the cable flew out with such force that it did not simply fall in a heap on the aft part of the ship. Rather, it shot out and away from the ship beyond the bulkhead and over the pier. The cable became a projectile as if the armature was a cannon.

Taking Straggler, tangled in a loop, with it.

Pulling Straggler through the top pulley.

In a high arc the cable sailed out onto the pier, the Russian beatnik in tow, arms waving helplessly, his beret and sunglasses close behind.

There was a shipping container blocking my view of the cable crunching down onto the pier.

Which it did with a stuttering *WHUMP*.

They assassinated King Max, and I did something about it.

I chased the beatniks down, and I nailed one of them.

Remarkable.

CHAPTER 11

MY CHASE OF THE ASSASSINS HAD UNINTENDED RESULTS. Namely, it made me even more adored by the populace. Not only had I endeared myself to the public with my speech at the testimonial dinner, but my stunt launching the boat over the earthen approach to the draw bridge was caught on dash cams from both directions.

Their king was dead, murdered, and they wept openly in the streets, portraits of His Majesty draped in black at every doorstep.

Ominously, the three who left Straggler vanished without a trace.

More ominous still, the police quickly identified and published a picture of Straggler. He was identified not a Russian, but an ethnically black Zarengi and known member of the Zarenga Liberation Front.

Perhaps one would imagine that I should have contradicted them, insisting that they were wrong and that the assassins were Russians? One might also imagine that I am becoming wiser about not blurting out everything I know, because in this case, I would be calling the police liars. This would indirectly assert their reasons for lying. Namely, that it was a frame up. Either the Russians or someone else had hired those four and the authorities were determined to blame it on the ZLF. And if I went public with what I knew, how long before my limo exploded?

Diabolical, really. It was easy for me to put the pieces together – the Kings Council wanted Max III out of the way but they also wanted to crush the ZLF, and they had sought to accomplish both in one deft swoop.

Could they really be so certain that they could get me to play along and not rock the boat, not push back, and just rubber stamp whatever they wanted? It's clearly why they bought my contract. Perhaps Prentis Hargreaves told them I would be putty in their hands.

It didn't matter. I was determined that I was not going to play along and I was not going to be coronated, for the simple fact that it was likely the King's Council or the Russians would murder me either way.

It was with these grim realities that the police escorted me back by squad car to my townhouse late that afternoon, which is, as we all know, cocktail hour.

My boat was to be returned the following day.

The street in front of my townhouse was still being cleared of debris from the explosions that morning, and when I stepped from the pintsize squad car, there were piles of jetsam from the explosion swept into small piles hither and yon, including beside the pathway to my door.

Numerous other small squad cars and even more security people had created a phalanx of cops around my digs, presumably to protect me from the ZLF. Still a gorgeous tropical day, the sun slanted through rustling palm fronds across my lawn and bits of debris. I bid the police goodbye, and tromped up the walkway with all the optimism of the condemned, my sandals clacking on the stone path.

Near the front door, one piece of debris caught my eye. It was shiny, and at first I thought nothing of it, just a snippet of chrome trim, part of some eyeglasses, or even an unidentified metal cylinder.

Sweat sprung to my brow.

My eyes zoomed in on the shiny object.

It was Max's titanium cylinder containing the thumb drive.

The explosion had flung it onto the lawn.

In a smooth, casual manner I scooped up the little cylinder and palmed it, hands swaying at my side so that it did not appear that I put anything in my pocket, consciously breathing slowly.

I walked toward my door, anticipating a shout behind me say: *Hey! What was that you picked up?*

At that moment, someone behind me shouted "Hey!"

The sweat on my brow went to frost. But I kept walking as if I had no idea they were talking to me.

"Hey!" A hand landed on my shoulder, and I turned, vision blurred.

It was Tanya. She said: "I have to check the premises one more time before you go in to make sure it is empty."

Trotting ahead, she pushed through the townhouse door, leaving it open.

Her comely shape reappeared in the doorway, and for whatever reason I was taken back to the first time I saw her magnificent breasts. Implants, mind you, but…anyhow, chalk it up to the indomitable male libido that at that moment of all moments I could summon a thought like that.

She waved me in.

As I passed her in the doorway I could smell her scent, which was like coconut for some reason. Maybe it was her shampoo, though when I stayed with her on her little sailboat in Nassau over Christmas I had not seen any such shampoo.

She closed the door behind me and we were alone.

The cylinder was secreted in my shorts pocket, and I continued around the breakfast bar to the mini bar.

What sort of cocktail does one have at a moment like that?

Ah, of course.

As luck would have it, the mini bar had VSOP brandy, gin, and ginger ale. There was no lime, but there was what appeared to be a bigarade – a sour orange, which would have to do.

The cocktail I had in mind was a famed old tiki

recipe that I had spent years fruitlessly researching and trying to perfect. Most accounts of its invention in a hotel bar in Cairo insist that it is made with both bourbon and gin. As such, I spent inordinate amounts of time with various proportions and no result was satisfactory. Some will disagree, but to me the flavor profile of gin and bourbon are too at odds to bring together into something that does not taste overwhelmingly like one or the other or nothing particularly good. Many will insist that adding bitters serves to blend the flavors, and it does change the flavor, just not in a way that makes it quantifiably better than gin or bourbon – not even when you add lime juice. Likely some 'mixologists' out there will insist I was not using the right bourbon or the correct gin. But accounts of the original recipe clearly indicate bourbon 'or brandy.' Or brandy? How is that interchangeable with bourbon except to a teetotaler?

Well, let me tell you, it makes a gigantic difference.

Did I neglect to mention the cocktail's name?

Suffering Bastard.

I gathered the ingredients and two glasses on the breakfast bar and said to Tanya: "Excuse me, security person, could you gather me some ice from the freezer?"

She did as I asked, and as she brought the ice, she sidled next to me, whispering: "We have to talk, but not here. Surveillance."

Propinquity is the precise word for what it felt to be near to her again, but I would not expect many to have this in their vocabulary, not the least my spin on the word. It certainly was not a word I knew until Conglamerated sent me to coaches to change Jersey Boone into Uptown Boone. Technically, *propinquity* can merely mean in close proximity. The broader meaning is the attraction that develops between two people who have been in close proximity. I take it a step further to mean the attraction between two people who have been intimate when they are once again in close proximity.

As we had been intimate just five months prior, and for a week's time, I sensed her warmth, her latent passion.

I said aloud. "Thank you, security person. Can I make you a cocktail?"

"Not while I'm working, sir." A flush to her cheek, she stepped away from me to the sliding glass doors where she peered suspisciously out at the happy blue bay.

"That's a shame you can't join me in a cocktail. This is a rare one called Suffering Bastard."

I filled a cloth napkin with ice, gathered the napkin at the four corners, and banged the ice on the edge of the counter:

BANG.

BANG.

BANG.

Tanya spun toward me from the window, gun drawn in a flash. An instant later, the front door flew open and more security spilled into the room, pistols drawn.

"It's OK, stand down." Tanya shouted. "He's just crushing ice."

Dirty looks favored me all around, to which I

responded: "What?"

As the troops piled back out the front door, Tanya said: "Sir, please don't make loud noises like that, we're on high alert."

I dumped the crushed ice from the towel into my glass, and went about quietly formulating my Suffering Bastard. Perversely, their reaction to my crushing ice amused me, as did Tanya's annoyance with my *savoir faire*. Under duress, nothing resets my composure like making a cocktail, and damn those who would disrupt that with their 'high alerts.'

As I stirred my drink in a pitcher, I took a moment to adjust my compsure to my situation. Whatever was on that thumb drive either could save me or sink me.

Yet they did not know I had it.

Knowledge, they tell me, is power. In this case, the lack of their knowledge was my power.

Alas, did they know that Max had the drive? Certainly if my place were bugged they did. They heard his every word.

And my every word. I hope they took them to heart. Unlikely. My manipulators never seem to care a wit about what I want. They just want to pull the strings.

What to do with the thumb drive? Tell Tanya, have her take it and get it to the proper channels to use it most effectively?

Use it to do what, though?

I wanted to plug the drive in and see what was on it. For the time being, it was my intent to keep that thumb drive as my ace in the hole.

With a flourish, I poured my Suffering Bastard and the ice crackled happily, like an audience of drunk Lilliputians applauding. I garnished with a peel of bigarade and turned toward Tanya, who leaned next to the sliding doors, arms folded, the plush lips askew and clearly peevish.

Approaching her, I said: "Can we go out onto the veranda, enjoy the late afteroon?"

She reached out and slid the door open, and I stepped past her into the salt air. Surveying the cobalt waters, I wondered if the King's assassination would mean I would not find an opportunity any time soon to fish. As Tanya stepped next to me, I likewise wondered whether she and I could spend any time alone together.

Raising an eyebrow at her, I whispered: "Can we talk here?"

"Yes." She looked away, whispering: "Wondering why I'm here?"

"Not at all." I supressed a laugh. "It isn't very difficult to figure out. Hard to imagine you came here on your own accord. You were sent here because of me. They borrowed you from the DEA because they feel you can handle me to do something in Zarenga Chi that serves the purposes of some agency or the other. That about the size of it?"

"Mm hm."

I squeezed my garnish and dropped it into my drink. "So what is it that the people you are working for want me to do?"

"Information. The King had some information on Russian investments in Zarenga Chi. We felt you might be able to get close to him, wanted you to make the deal and have him hand over what he's got. But now..."

The metal cylinder in my pocket fairly pulsed.

"Investments?"

"We believe this is where Putin has hidden all the money he has looted from his country. Hundreds of billions of dollars. Maximillian had the goods and had reached out to us to see if we would protect his Monarchy in exchange for the information. Possibly support the ZLF if the King's Council refused to clean house and call for elections."

I wanted to say: *Ah, support the ZLF by passing them Miranda's name to lure me into a kidnapping?*

Instead I said: "Oh, really? Support the tiny ZLF against this multinational behemoth? Against Putin?"

Folding her arms, she cocked her head at me. "Like we haven't made similar deals? Come on, Boone."

"And what happens to the native Zarengis? Likely they don't count for much in their figuring."

"Don't be naïve. That's the world we live in, Boone." Her whisper was bitter.

My mind began to shuffle the playing cards of this fine messy racket, looking for a winning hand. Yet the deck seemed half jokers, with at least one king, the one with a sword through his head.

"So now that Max is dead, what is it your people

want me to do?"

She took a deep breath and let it out slowly, whispering: "Ascend to the throne. If Max could find this information from that high perch, so can you."

I chuckled without humor, wagging my head. "Why does this fall all on me? Aren't the NSA and other shadowy organizations exhorbitantly funded enough? Don't they have the super computers, satelites, PEGBOTS..."

"PEGBOTS?"

"Never mind...these agencies supposedly have all this expensive, sophisticated gear and butler spies and all manner of operatives and yet in the clinches its me they need? I don't suppose that they give my well-being any more thought than that of the Zarengis facing a civil war."

"You know, you do seem to have a unique talent for putting yourself in the middle. You are heir to the throne, you know."

I snorted. "Ah, so it's all my fault, is it? And it's all about thwarting the Russians, too? You know, those were not ZLF who assassinated King Max. When I chased them down, I cornered one, and he was wearing grease paint to look black. He and the others cursed in Russain."

I saw her cheeks pale. "You told this to the constabulary?"

"I did not."

"Why?"

"When they claimed it was someone else, and were covering it up… I've learned, you sometimes want them to think you don't know what you know."

"What?"

"Or have them not know what you know. I think if they knew I knew it was not the ZLF and was in fact Russians that assassinated Max then my life would hang from a string." I sipped my drink. First rate, I got the balance just right, and the sour of the bigarade really set off the ginger flavors. "This drink is fantastic, if I do say so."

"Boone, you have to take your situation very seriously. They might think that you know it was Russians. They may know you know they are covering it up and therefore you know they are complicit with the Russians."

"Ah, but they don't *actually* know. They may suspect. And they suspect a great deal. They suspect I'm an idiot who will become their puppet king. They have no interest in anything but using me to their ends."

Her eyes were behind sunglasses, so I couldn't see them directly just from the side, and I saw her lashes blink rapidly.

"You should know by now, Boone, that the government doesn't perceive its best interests as yours or anybody's but their own."

"So the Russians seem to be in on this plot to make me King, they are in cahoots with our people from what I can see. How does that work? Is the U.S. actually trying to expose Putin's operation or protect him?"

"Protect him?"

"Now whose being naïve? Twisty loyalties are not the sole province of spy agencies. The Russian reach is like a kraken's tentacles around our nation's frigate – Putin's subversion is all over the newspapers."

"It doesn't matter," she whispered angrily, her fists on the railing. "I have a job to do." I sensed her frustration with her predicament: she wasn't sure what she was doing and for whom. Or why.

So she veered away from the subject at hand. "I really don't understand how you manage to get yourself in such a mess all the time. And constantly hearing that you're dead. What we had in Nassau...look, we're too different, Boone. We're on different paths."

Gazing into the distance, past the bay and into the deep blue ocean horizon, I suspected she was probably right, that there was no going back to Nassau. Some relationships flower only briefly. But still... *propinquity*.

I wanted to put my hand on hers, but did not. They may not be listening, but they might be watching.

They. Them. I've come to live in a world of powers-that-be, manipulators in some far-off 'situation room' deciding what they want me to do next.

Another thing I had learned from my entanglements with espionage was that what 'they' didn't know was in my favor.

Number One: the thumb drive.

Number Two: I know the assassins were Russian.

Number Three: Foresh.

Lovely Foresh could be important. Perhaps I could get her to transport the data from the thumb drive overseas.

Of course, I hoped Tanya didn't know about her.

"And Boone, what was that with the flight attendant?"

Damn.

Men: when confronted, never say 'what was what?' Or worse, 'Who?' Women interpret that as an admission of guilt. Why, I don't know. Likely as not, men instictively say that when they are prevaricating. The trick is to take a moment to collect your thoughts, looking puzzled.

And to always tell the truth.

Mostly.

"You mean, Foresh? Yes, nice kid."

She turned to look at me. Head cocked. "I'll bet."

"We played a board game to kill some time on the long flight. Are you trying to insinuate something?"

"On her way past you at the airport she smiled at you."

I sipped my drink. "Why, Tanya, I believe jealousy is getting the better of you. It was an innocent smile. Was she supposed to ignore me? Frown at me?"

Color came to her cheek. "You don't know that she isn't working for someone else."

"We all work for someone."

We heard the front door open and turned from the porch railing to see who was entering.

From the relative gloom of the living room, an old gentleman in a seersucker suit and flowing white hair, approached, swinging a cane from one hand. His kindly wrinkles scrunched into a smiling face behind his round wire specs. Last I'd seen him was the night I'd been shot through the ear, with Noomba in the limo.

Sliding the door open, Linus Trimble stepped out on to the porch and pointed the silver handle of his cane. "Tanya, you can go."

Tanya ducked through the door and out.

In his gravelly southern drawl he said: "I suppose you didn't expect to see me again so soon. Well, in all candor, I did not expect to see you again so soon either, sir."

I laughed softly, shaking my head at the ground and the devil below. "I've learned to expect the unexpected, Linus. I thought you were with the Justice Department – what are you doing here?"

"Technically, I work for the Department of Commerce, National Institute of Standards and Technology. But I work for all kinds of agencies."

"Of course you do, I should have guessed. And of course you're the one who put Tanya up to running me." Same U.S. 'institute' that was manipulating me in Russia. I gazed at all the sleek condos across the bay, sided by palm trees and profusions of flowers. The bay water was gem blue, and shoals of minnows flashed in the late day sun. In the distance, gaudy hot air balloons sailed across a deep blue sky toward the summit of the volcano, Mumu.

Zarenga Chi was a stunning, luxuriant island. It was hard to imagine it becoming a war zone, a sea of smoldering town houses, the air filled with smoke, the smell of burning tires and the intermittent eruption of gunfire.

Trimble ignored my last comment, surveying his immediate surroundings until he found a striped patio chair, which he slid forward and settled his bulk into with a satisfied gasp. "An unfortunate turn of events for King Max. And a remarkable turn of events that you chased down his killers. Were they Russian?"

Now I looked to the sky and beyond to whatever beneficent powers might be lurking there. Moments like this made me doubt anybody was home.

"You know they were Russian, so why are you asking me?"

His laugh was a nearly soundless wheeze, his barrel chest undulating.

"Tanya tell you why we want you here?"

"She did."

"It would seem Putin wants you king as much as we do, but for different reasons."

Really?

"You want me to get the goods on Putin, and Putin wants me under his thumb, to be his pet poodle and keep the realm stable and keep his fortune hidden. That your story?"

"That, sir, is a fair assessment."

"And the King's Council? They run this place, so they're the ones who had the police cover up the true identity of the assassins."

"They are in Putin's pocket."

"They must know what you're up to."

"They think the United States of America's sole intent is helping with their terrorist problem, and keeping the country and its industries stable."

"And so somehow all the players here have figured out that the solution to their problems is me?"

He chuckled. "As they say, it isn't as if this is the first time. You lead a charmed life, Mr. Linsenbigler."

"Well, that's a bunch of malarkey, and everybody is going to have to find a solution to their problems without Ol' Boonie."

He admired the silver handle of his cane, which was cast in the shape of a fox's head. "Now, if you decline to ascend to the Zarengi throne, one solution the Council and Putin might choose would be your demise. No more heir to the throne would give the King's Council the excuse they need to impose autocratic rule. Obviously, this is not their first choice or they never would have bought your contract. They fear an uprising and the ZLF."

"Wouldn't that look kind of suspicious, hot on the heels of King Max's assassination?"

He pursed his lips. "Another option is that you become king. Not so bad to be king! You'd be rich and not have to do much but cocktail and fish and entertain, though they'd want you to sire children legitimately, of course. They need heirs. You'd live in the palace by the sea with the best stocked bar in the southern hemisphere. You'd have the royal yacht at your disposal to fish anytime you please. Hard to imagine a better alternative for a man of your appetites and proclivities."

"A gilded cage?" I snorted. "Not for me. Why can't I just decline? They could simply tell their people I said no and then figure something else out that doesn't include an uprising. Perhaps sit down with the ZLF and hammer out some sort of representative government."

He smiled, mostly to himself. "You could try saying no. But then what? Amalgamated Consumables doesn't really need you as a shill for their products – they have a virtual monopoly already in place throughout Africa. Assuming they would be willing to surrender control of the government to the citizenry? (And that's a big fat assumption.) Well, more than likely, they'd send you packing and you'd fade into obscurity, a has-been, your reputation forever in tatters as a result of that Russian episode."

"I wouldn't mind living out of the limelight, believe me."

He chuckled. "You know, Boone, my daddy would often say that big decisions are best made after a day commanding a pole at his favorite fishing hole. They have some fine offshore fishing here in Zarenga Chi. What say you and I head out tomorrow morning and see what leviathans we can pull up from the deep blue fathoms?"

Well, I had to hand it to Linus, he knew where I lived, either in a bottle of bourbon or on a boat with a rod in my hand. In a grim way, I also appreciated the fact that he wasn't prepared just to barge in and hit me with the hard sell. You know, your *country needs you* and *this is important.*

He was going to take his time and romance me into becoming king.

I faced him, arms folded across my chest.

"You're on."

CHAPTER 12

MY EVENING WAS BLISSFULLY UNEVENTFUL. Nobody came to see me, nobody barged in, and nobody assaulted me or blew anything or anybody up nearby – that I knew of.

I was perfectly happy to spend the evening playing with my tackle.

Ahem, well, perhaps that sounded metaphoric: I was assembling my fishing rods, putting line through the guides and attaching leaders and flies. My gear bags needed some organization, and I wanted to unpack and choose what togs I would wear the following day.

Once that was accomplished, it was night, the lights of the condos sparkling on the water.

Mind you, I had no sooner awoken that morning than I had been confronted by the King, took chase after some Russian beatniks, played patty cake with the police for a few hours before tromping home and being compelled to have not one but two spook sessions.

I was ripe for a shower and shave, finalized with a

trim of my signature whiskers.

Clean white shirt and tropical chinos completed the transformation.

In the process, I had secreted my small laptop into the steamy bathroom, where I plugged in the silver thumb drive. I doubted that the bathroom was under surveillance, but even if it was, the lens would certainly have been fogged.

The drive contained numerous PDFs of Zarengi National Bank records for numerous Russian monopolies like Gazprom. The records indicated huge balances and deposits. Skipping down, there were other PDFs depicting transfers to other accounts under other companies. Swiss and Luxembourgian accounts in the name of someone named Roldugin showed huge transfers from Bank Rossiya. From the same bank, transfers by its president Kovalchuk, on behalf of Vladimir Putin. There was another document that indicated that Bank Rossiya had purchased controlling shares in the Zarengi National Bank.

As I am hard pressed to keep on top of my personal credit card bills and account balances, I could not forensically dissect what all this meant, and I was only glancing at a fraction of the documents on the thumb drive.

Yet I was able to surmise that what the drive contained was a boatload of financial documents regarding Russian investments in the Zarengi National Bank. And that the Russians were moving money from their banks into the ZNB and then from there to another offshore bank in Zarengi currency. I believed that what the drive contained was evidence that Zarenga Chi had become a major money laundering center as well as Putin's personal piggy bank. I did not see whether there were any ties to American businessmen, but there could have been.

It would seem that Max did, indeed, have the goods.

Now that it was in my possession, I personally had the ability – responsibility? – to ensure that this information was placed into the hands of those who could do the most good with it.

No doubt, many in my position would simply have handed the silver drive over to Tanya, or Trimble. This was what they were after, wasn't it? Then I could just go on my merry way and they would leave me alone.

That's the world we live in, Boone.

Tanya's words, and the cynicism, echoed.

This was not my first rodeo and I knew that I could not entirely trust anyone who was vested in gamesmanship with Putin and piles and piles of money.

In my laptop case I had three black thumb drives, and I copied the silver drive onto all of them. Why? I did not want all my rum in one shaker. It might be that the silver drive became lost, or someone stole it, or someone made me give it to them in exchange for my life.

One of the black thumb drives I placed into an envelope from the desk and squeezed it between the wall and the padded bedstead. The other two I placed in small zip seal plastic sleeves that held fishing leaders. One of those I put in my fishing kit, and the other I slid into the bottom of a rod tube. I did all this knowing I might be watched so acted as though I were further organizing my fishing gear.

The titanium cylinder with the original drive went around my neck even as it had Max's.

I had eaten little that day and so was borderline famished. The fridge contained cured meats, cheeses, black olives and a baguette, which with the help of a large dinner plate I fashioned into an antipasto platter. I garnished the plate with some of the odd bitter fruit I'd consumed that morning.

Suffering Bastards do not pair well with food – well, perhaps pu-pu platters.

Perusing the liquor cabinet, I came upon Cocchi Americano (a bitter Italian aperitif), gin and triple sec. I usually disdain triple sec in favor of finer orange flavored spirits (Dry Curacao in particular) but I had to cast at the fish in front of me. I substituted a slice of bitter orange for lemon, and a few drops of ouzo for the dash of absinthe as there was none of the latter in the bar.

On the porch over the water, I lit up some tiki torches and sat in the striped chair where Trimble had brandished the smile of the Cheshire cat. I admired my drink by the torch light and took her for a spin. The cocktail was a nice take on a classic named Corpse Reviver #2.

If only it could revive King Max.

As such, I toasted his memory.

I dined on dried sausage, cheese, hunks of bread and the occasional briny olive. This was the time to consider my next move, and what the variables were. Lord knows I'd rather have been trying to figure out what fly to float in what seam in a river for a monster trout, but getting myself out of this mess, and figuring out how to use the drive to do so, required careful consideration.

One: I had to consider what was on the thumb drive and who should get it and why. When that information came out, what would happen to Zarenga Chi?

Two: what was going to happen to Zarenga Chi without a king? With the monarchy dissolved, and the corporations in full control, would the small island nation devolve into a complete oligarchy? Would they crush the ZLF? Or would the ZLF gain momentum and launch a revolution?

Three: was the United States going to back the ZLF and support a civil uprising against an oligarchy, which they know is Putin's financial bastion?

Four: since when did I involve myself in any politics of any kind? How was it my responsibility – someone with no political or diplomatic experience, leanings or inclinations – supposed to know how to try to influence considerations one, two or three? It had been my general opinion that world events have a life of their own and that to try to influence them or reverse them was one of humankind's greatest conceits.

Yet for some odd reason it mattered to me what

happened to all those people at the airport. I avoid watching the news yet am bombarded by it at airports and bars. You don't have to watch much of it to witness what civil strife has done to what were once thriving and vital cities and towns.

Sipping my corpse reviver, I admired the pretty harbor and all the twinkling lights. Above was a blaze of stars, and a light breeze rustled the palms.

Inasmuch as the U.S. knew that Putin had his stash here, and was laundering illicit money through the Zarengi treasury, the cat was out of the bag already, wasn't it? Trimble and his lot just wanted the proof, the account numbers, and the names. But would they actually make the information public or did they maybe want the Russians to know they had it but not use it? To let the Russians know they knew and effectively use it as blackmail to attain some other end result?

Absurd. Perhaps.

Then again, the 'great game' of espionage is often counterintuitive.

I subscribe to Thoreau's view that simplicity should govern decisions.

If I released the information to the press, then everybody would know what the other guy knows.

In point of fact, *everybody would know.*

Putin would know.

The U.S. would know.

Zarengis would know.

The ZLF would know.

This guileless approach allowed me to wash my hands of it. Nobody was given any advantage and it was up to the players to sort it out. Argue with my calculus if you wish, but that's the only way ol' Boonie knew how to slice this lemon.

A great sigh of relief: that's that.

Yet as I took another sip of my tangy reviver, the matter of how to transmit the information to the press was a problem. I did not dare to try to send the information through the internet. If they had surveillance in my apartment, it was likely they would monitor my electronic transmissions. To include my phone.

I had to get one of the drives back to the States.

Somehow. Foresh might work if I could locate her.

Then there was Terry, my former publicist.

I fired up my phone, and it took a while for it to realize where we were now. Similar to the time I switched it on in Kazakhstan, the phone finally played a little fanfare and announced 'WELCOME TO ZARENGA CHI!'

Of course, I was also informed that transmissions to another country would cost a small fortune, but I began to text Terry Orbach anyway. Cognizant that my message would likely be read by prying eyes, I divulged nothing of my actual predicament.

Terry, I think there may be some genuine opportunities to rebuild my brand back in the US if you come down here. You should be able to get a business visa. Let me know.

Perhaps I wasn't lying.

CHAPTER 13

MY SHIMMERING BLUE FLY SAILED through the air and slapped down in the froth of the boat's wake. A native Zarengi stood next to me, the boat's mate, Ando. Rod in hand, he reeled furiously to retrieve a hookless blue teaser lure he'd used to raise the striped marlin, its long bill slashing at the water surface from below.

Stripping my fly in rapidly across the water surface, I hoped to draw the fish's attention and have it give chase.

The mate Ando put a hand on my arm: "Stop!"

I did so, my heart thumping in my ears, my vision blurred with excitement and anticipation.

This had been the third billfish that I had cast to that day. One of the others I hooked briefly and he threw the fly on the first jump. The second hated my fly and vanished.

I stood on the aft angling deck of a thirty-five foot convertible fishing boat. It had a tall flybridge and elevated helm from which the skipper kept the boat moving slowly. The dark blue of the sea twinkled with fingers of sunlight, skies clear except for a small flock of terns following the boat hoping for stray baitfish.

Directly behind me in the shade were Trimble and Kinkaid perched in captain's chairs. Linus was in turquoise beach togs and orange flip-flops, his mole-ridden skin likely having not seen the sun in many years. Yet he sat there with his flowing white hair and round sunglasses as if he were Neptune himself. My new boss Kinkaid had gone the opposite route, a man of rock rigged in a yachting outfit: white pants, white shirt, blue monogrammed blazer, and topped with a white yachtsman's cap.

Stripped to the waist, I wore only sunglasses, shorts, a fighting belt, gloves and ample sunscreen.

A black sword suddenly lanced the froth next to my fly.

"Wait!" Ando shouted. "Don't move."

The black sword sank beneath the froth, replaced by the end of the fish's tail as it turned away. I couldn't be sure if he merely sunk my fly or if he had eaten it.

Then I noticed my flyline moving rapidly away from me.

"Now!" the mate shouted.

Fly rod hard to starboard, I reeled furiously and yanked sideways with my entire torso – enacted with all the gusto of a whaler harpooning a whale.

With the crack of a whip the line went taught, and thirty yards of line shot off my screaming reel.

Four boat lengths back, a striped marlin shot high

out of the water, my fly in its beak. Kinkaid and Trimble roared with approval.

The captain shifted the boat into reverse, and we began to follow the fish as it rocketed off farther starboard.

I watched as more line vanished from my reel – I worried that I might get 'lined', or run out of line and have it snap off the reel.

The captain anticipated my concern and sped the boat faster after the fish, which once more exploded from the surface of the sea and cartwheeled back down with an enormous splash.

"Boone, start to pressure him," Ando whispered.

With a gloved palm, I applied pressure to the outer rim of the reel to limit the amount of line I would allow the fish to take. Now I had to hope that the fish's sword had not nicked the heavy leader, and that the line near the striped marlin's mouth would not surrender to the added strain.

Sweat stung my eyes as it coursed down my brow, my biceps taught and tingling. The boat rose and fell with the gentle chop, backwash topping the gunnels and dowsing my shorts.

Two more jumps – the second one not even fully out of the water – and then we knew the fish was tiring. I was putting line back on the reel. Ando told me what I had already read: "Boone, when he come close to boat, it not over, so don't pressure him too much. If you do, he will jump in the boat with us, and you and I have to jump out of the boat so we don't die. You understand? Tell me you understand, because my wife will kill me if I die."

I grinned at the joke. "Understood!"

With most of the line back on the reel, the fish suddenly sounded below the boat, ripping off line again.

The captain switched off the engines.

"That OK," Ando said with obvious approval. "This good. Now we just have to hope the knots hold and leader don't break. If the hook was gonna break, it would have happened with the jumps. Keep the pressure on, Boone, this the home stretch." He began to put on heavy landing gloves and goggles. In videos of this enterprise, I had not seen any mates wear goggles but he explained earlier that without them he risked getting stabbed in the eye when he reached down to land the fish by grasping its sword. If the fish suddenly surged or thrashed while he was leaning over it, I could see how easily that could occur.

Moving with the direction of the fish, I shuffled from one side of the boat to the other. When I peered down into the dark blue, I could sometimes make out the silvery side of the fish. I knew that was good, he was seriously tired now and turning sideways instead of swimming to resist being brought to the surface.

Ando clapped his gloves together and gave me a big smile, eyebrows dancing atop his bright blue eyes. "You ready, Boone?"

I nodded, conscious that my biceps were aching in protest of this abuse.

The mate turned to Kinkaid and Trimble. "You gentlemen ready with the cameras? Take as many photos as you can as fast as possible leaning over the side that we land on. Fill the frame with Boone and the fish. I'm gonna be very mad if we don't get good photos of Boone's first marlin fishy."

The two duffers chuckled at his insolence and began to ready their cell phones.

As I hauled the fish up from the deep, my legs had now joined my biceps in protest of this exploit, my kneecaps trembling and calves burning.

The dark shape of the fish got larger and larger as I hauled back on the rod and then reeled down again, over and over. It seemed to take forever, and the dread of losing the fish began to haunt me. Imagine after all that to lose the fish! I could picture a knot, in close up, fraying, bucking. I could picture the hook almost bent straight, the flesh in which it was imbedded torn and about to give way. More than once I closed my eyes, for all intents, praying that nothing would go wrong.

Steady, old man, we're just about there, keep your resolve, and above all else, don't rush it at the end! You can do this.

The dark shape became bigger, enough so that I began to realize how gigantic the fish was, and now my dread was turning to fright. This fish was bigger than I was, and unlike me, it was armed with a deadly weapon.

There are horrendous stories of sailfish or marlin lunging over the bow of the boat and lancing men straight through the chest. I had read about such an incident where the fish went back over the hull with the man stuck on its beak like a cocktail onion on a toothpick. When this fish sounded, it took the man with him to Davey Jones locker. Yet the man somehow managed to slide himself off the sword and return to the surface. I believe he survived this catastrophe, too!

Eyes closed, I laughed to myself, becoming giddy from the strain on mind and body.

Imagine that – what a way to go, after all. Of all the ways I have almost been killed, to die that way would be a relative honor!

With the great fish moving from one side of the boat to the other, it began to turn on its side again, the two-tone blue and silver flanks barred in white with blue dots.

Finally, Ando said: "Show time. Step back and let me grab the leader. When I have him alongside by the sword, I will cut the leader. You reel up quick and come next to me, rod out where it can be seen. Boone don't want nobody to think he used bait and a fighting chair after all this, right? Gentlemen, be ready with those cameras. With forced flash!"

Moments later, Ando's hand was on the leader and he drew the fish near enough that he could grab ahold of the sword – and when he did so the exhausted fish thrashed only a little before going still alongside the boat.

In days of yore, a boated fish was summarily hoisted up by its tail for photos, but that would kill the fish, and the practice nowadays is to release them to fight another day. As such, the mate holds the fish alongside the boat in the water, and the angler comes in next to him. They are photographed together with the fish still in the water, the mate raising the fish slightly for the camera.

There I was next to the mate laughing with utter exhaustion, the eye of the great fish staring at us in what looked like wonder. A bright orange stripe had appeared between the upper blue part of the fish, and the triangular dorsal fin was deep purple. Billfish change color while fighting and when subdued.

Kinkaid and Trimble leaned over the gunnel with their phones and snapped away, the little flashes on the devices twinkling.

Ando used plyers to pluck the fly from the fish's jaw and said: "Thank you, marlin fishy, and let this be a lesson to you. Stay away from boats!"

His gloved hand released the sword and the fish sank down, the long black shape straight and unmoving. When it was about twenty feet down, the tail thrashed once, and the marlin angled down and out of sight.

I like all kinds of fishing – in streams and lakes and surf and back bays and lagoons and tidal flats. It's all technically and athletically challenging.

Yet there's a special kind of exhilaration you get from being physically and emotionally challenged by fishing that is over the top. You win the day by blood and guts endurance, by buckling down, by staying focused, and being smart about using your legs and weight to fight the fish, not your back or arms. You win the day by not blowing it when you are utterly drained and wondering why this is fun.

My first striped marlin left me feeling exhilarated. First off, a large fish that jumps repeatedly at the end of your line is thrilling, and the long runs dramatic.

I hugged Ando, practically weeping, and he laughed in my ear and said. "So you wanna do that again? Let's go find another striped marliny!"

The fat man in the togs and the yachtsman clapped me on the back, lauding my accomplishment with hearty guffaws and *well dones*.

Ando began washing down the deck with a hose and I clapped him on the shoulder. "Thank you, Ando. I think I'm done for today. But time permitting, I'd like to go out tomorrow for wahoo. Always wanted to catch one."

He grinned and rolled his eyes. "Oh, you want to catch the devil, do you? There's a fishy you don't want in the boat while he's still with any life!"

I returned to the shade where my compatriots had taken their seats. From a bucket of ice next to them, Kinkaid produced a cold bottle of Bindu, the local pilsner, and handed it out to me. When I took the icy bottle he searched his chair and the floor around him: "Now where is that opener?"

"Never mind," I said, reaching into the bucket of ice for a plastic bottle of water. Inverting the water bottle over the beer bottle, I locked the edge of the former's cap under the latter's cap and pried against my thumb. The beer bottle cap snapped off and flew into the sea.

They laughed with wonder at the ingenuity and deftness of this technique, one I had learned from the guides in Honduras. Trimble said: "There is never so dire a need as the need for a bottle opener on a hot day. Well done!"

We toasted, glass clinking, and I sank into a seat catty-corner to them, snatching a white terry towel from a wall hook and wrapping it around my neck. The sweat continued to cascade down my head and torso, and the malty Bindu was pure iced ambrosia, a veritable tonic for body and soul after fighting and landing that remarkable fish.

We sat in relative silence – that is, without saying anything as the boat's motor thrummed and the sea sloshed against the hull. The terns following the boat had given up hope and were gone, the azure sky underscored with the horizon of deep blue ocean. If only this, I mused, could be what every day was like.

But no.

Trimble sipped his beer and cleared his throat. "Boone, you've been through a lot these last couple days. You earned that fish." His southern drawl seemed thicker somehow than before. "I like to think that life isn't so much a series of events and eventualities, that there are tests the Almighty lays before us on our way to our destiny."

Here we go.

I shook my head, smiling. "The answer is no. Today, tomorrow, the day after that. No."

Kinkaid dove in with his gravelly brogue, his forearms resting on his knees, beer bottle cradled between. "I respect that, Boone, I honestly do. And I believe there's an exclusion in your contract with Amalgamated regarding any kind of political affiliation to keep your brand free of any allegiances that might tarnish the brand in any given market."

I said: "Thank you, Dermot, you cut me to the quick. While I'm all yours for two years and change, there's nothing in the contract compelling me to be king of Zarenga Chi. I wish you both would realize the patent insanity of that notion."

Linus's mouth curled into his Cheshire cat's smile as he said: "Come now, what is a king or a queen but a brand ambassador? Without an heir ascending to the throne and providing stability and inspiration, the everyday Zarengis you spoke of in your speech are going to start to side more heavily with the ZLF against the King's Council, which at this juncture is lacking a mandate to rule."

Sipping my beer, I squinted at the horizon. "And how is it that nobody foresaw this possibility?"

Kinkaid growled: "King Max wouldn't have it. He was paranoid, he thought we wanted to have him sign over the monarchy in the event of his death and then kill him. So here we are with no legal instrument to transfer power."

"Except you, sir," Trimble added.

Oh, what a nasty bunch of characters. When they

realized Max would not cooperate, they figured they could only afford to kill him once I was lined up and ready to go.

Perhaps the most insidious aspect to my predicament on that hot day on the rolling ocean was the thought that I was Putin's pawn again, that he himself had taken my chess piece and slid it forward on the checkered board. That perhaps Putin had lured me to the Russian Far East a few short months ago to somehow lay the foundation for making me the King of Zarenga Chi. The reasoning, the logic, the calculus was not altogether apparent, but from personal experience, I knew that Putin possessed a certain diabolical genius that was hard for mere mortals to understand or fathom. Had he lured me expressly to Russia to blow up fish, knowing that releasing film of that would ruin my career and that in turn I would be available for purchase by Amalgamated and ascend the throne of Zarenga Chi as his tool?

I think what flummoxes world leaders and diplomatic forecasters about Putin is that he sees world affairs as a fun game, and is not beyond geopolitical pranks that he does just to amuse himself. Yet always with a dark, fickle purpose.

I lifted my gaze from my glistening beer bottle to my compatriots. "And why not declare that elections take place within the year? Start the process of democratization?"

"The King's Council doesn't believe that's the best way to go forward." Kinkaid stood, grabbing an overhead rail to steady himself. "How many countries have tried democracy and failed? You get a tin-pot dictator in here looting the coffers, levying huge taxes on the corporations here, and then they leave, and Zarenga Chi is no longer able to revert to a sustenance way of life, food runs short, riots, a brutal dictator wreaking vengeance on the populace. You get the picture?"

I nodded and he continued.

"The King's Council firmly believes that what we have in Zarenga is something unique in the world. This is a nation that is taking another route, one better than democracy because the way we have it set up, level, corporate minds are at the helm. You're never going to have some populist demagogue take the reins here and drive the cart into the gulley. Look at all we've built, all we've done, the infrastructure…with all due respect to your native country, and Linus's, I don't think democracy is the answer to providing citizens with a high standard of living and the pursuit of happiness. Corporations, by their very profit-centric nature are efficient entities – unlike governments with bloated bureaucracies and do-nothing politicians."

"So Zarengis are really your employees not your citizens?"

"Semantics don't change the fact that we're the wealthiest country not only in Africa but in the world, and with a very high standard of living."

After a pause, I sipped my beer and grinned. *Don't take the bait, Boone. You're not political. This is not your game.*

From my tackle bag on the deck next to my chair I fished out my cigar case and offered the gentlemen a cigar – Linus took one, Kinkaid demurred. I fired up Trimble and then myself. Linus eyes the dark brown wrapper and corked shape of his cheroot.

"Boone, I don't believe I've seen a cigar like this before. It's sort of twisted, corkscrewed."

I nodded, blowing a stream of smoke that the breeze snatched and whisked away. "These are culebras. They come three twisted together. I have them made for me by Cubans in North Jersey. You approve?"

He nodded, and sipped from a beer bottle. "They draw quite nicely considering that they are bent."

I looked from my cigar to the rock-like features of Kinkaid under that white yachting hat, the boat's motor thrumming and hull rocking as we motored toward port.

Finally, I said: "Dermot, you own me, and I think your countrymen like me already even though I haven't done a single commercial yet or made an appearance at any trade shows. Likely your promotions people have a lot to work with in pushing my brand and any sorts of cocktail amenities you want to put my name to – assuming that's why you brought me here. Put me on a plane and have me cut the ribbon to new shopping malls, bars, nightclubs, whatever you like, all across your distribution zones. Run me ragged for the next two and a half years and get your money's worth. I have amply proved my marketability in the Northern Hemisphere, and as long as nobody in the Southern Hemisphere has a problem with me having once blown up some Russian fish with a grenade, there's no reason I can't be a gold mine for Amalgamated Consumables. Boone Linsenbigler as a brand is a known quantity. So what makes you think that Boone Linsenbigler would make a good king? So let's stick to me being a brand and not a monarch – that way you know what you're getting. I'm happy, you're happy."

He hung his head, and said to his shoes. "Very well. But can the Council count on you to participate in the funeral of Maximillian III? As his closest and only living male relative?"

By gadfrey! I'd won!

They'd given up on trying to make me king.

"Whatever ceremonial task you have for me to perform at Max's funeral I would be happy to oblige."

Kinkaid and Trimble shared a smile before he said. "We're much obliged."

CHAPTER 14

FLOWERS AND PORTRAITS OF KING MAX carpeted the lawn of my townhouse instead of little piles of debris. Well-wishers and distraught citizens had flocked to my residence to bestow upon me tokens of their grief and respect for King Max. The phalanx of security blockading the street had allowed people one by one to pass through the gauntlet to place their bouquets, ribbons and portraits of Max on the grass. My security detail – to include Tanya – led me up the sidewalk to my door. I marveled at the volume of it all, and the display made me feel a little guilty for having gone fishing. The citizens of Zarenga Chi were really torn up over this – I'm not sure why that surprised me, but I didn't expect their condolences to be directed at me.

I felt guilt for not having been there to receive these tokens, but also for not stepping up to help them, become their king, accept their adoration and do what I could to help them and protect them from becoming just employees. Yet at the same time, I knew that to do so would not go well. That's not who I was, even if I wanted to be a leader of men and champion of the poor. I'm simply not crafty enough or shrewd and discerning enough to lead a country. I don't have the aptitude for it, and I certainly would not be happy as the idiot king and puppet of the King's Council and Putin.

What I could do for the native Zarengi was make sure that the thumb drive found its way to the press back in the States. Perhaps if that information freed the King's Council from Putin's control, they would consider some sort of representative government.

Tanya did not come inside with me, and I admit to being a little relieved that she did not. More lectures on what I should do were not welcome – I had already run through the options and my conscience, and knew what needed to be done.

Showered and shaved, I dressed in chinos and a tribal blue Hawaiian shirt. On my way downstairs I checked my phone. No message from Terry.

Orange light of the fading day lit up the living room, and as I turned the corner of the breakfast bar I was still looking at my phone.

In my peripheral vision: someone sitting in the rattan wing chair by the sliding glass doors to the porch.

Startled, my heart jumped, and so did my legs, stools at the breakfast bar toppling as I recoiled.

"Foresh!" I gasped in disbelief.

"I'm sorry! I did not mean to frighten you!" She

jumped to her feet and trotted over to help me right the bar stools.

I said: "I'm surprised they let you in here." Her scent of green apple gave me a quick and naughty flashback.

"They did not let me in here. I swam under your dock into your boathouse. I hope you do not mind that I put on one of your shirts." Again, I could not be sure by her lilting tone whether she was being facetious, as if any man would be upset that a lovely girl in a bikini (with whom he'd enjoyed an induction into the Mile High Club) suddenly showed up and put on one of your shirts.

She wore my yellow fishing shirt over her orange bikini, and her long dark hair was wet and swept to the side of her blue eyes. I know it may seem odd – confronted with a lively girl in a bikini – to note once again how lovely her dark skin was. In the orange sunlight she was practically glowing.

"Foresh, what inspired you to swim under my dock and risk being arrested by security?"

She put a hand on my cheek, her eyes searching mine. "You almost got killed by terrorists and now they say you will be king of Zarenga Chi. I had to see you to know that you are fine and what you will do. A girl doesn't often find a new lover who will become a king, or one in so much danger. I am flying out tomorrow, to New York, so wanted to see you before I left."

For a moment, I thought about the wisdom of Foresh staying at my abode for any length of time for fear that Tanya might suddenly make an appearance.

But Foresh was going to New York. She could be my courier.

Well, there was nothing for it, was there? Tanya expected me to do what's right for the country, for whichever country. She may have had another idea about what the 'right thing' might entail, but it was up to me in my predicament and my moral compass to do what was proper and make sure that the thumb drive got into the hands of journalists who would make the best use of it. As anyone can tell you, I am a paradigm of self-sacrifice. Not really, but if the sacrifice entails making love to a beautiful girl, that's not my fault.

I took Foresh's lovely hand from my cheek and clasped it. "You're right, there might be people who are trying to kill me, keep me from becoming King of Zarenga Chi. You gave me quite the start sneaking in here, but I'm glad you came. Can you stay for a glass of champagne?"

"I brought a fish for dinner. I speared it under your dock. It's in the sink. Yet...it is still early for dinner."

I guided her to the bar fridge and retrieved a bottle of what turned out to be Prosecco. "But it is cocktail hour."

She pouted at the floor, then batted her eyes at me. "You do not want to please me?"

With my free fingers of the hand holding the bottle, I snagged two champagne flutes and gestured toward the stair to the bedroom. "Well, we can do both, can't we?"

She didn't budge. "Here?"

With her free hand she hooked a thumb in her bikini

bottoms and wiggled them down to her feet, stepping out of them, her neatly trimmed tuck just visible between the yellow shirttails.

Imagine if Tanya had walked in mere moments later?

Another first: making love on a bar stool.

All for King and country...

CHAPTER 15

Julius Caesar's gigantic funeral pyre nearly burned down the forum.

Pharaoh Tutankhamun had a funerary procession to his tomb that was miles long.

Chinese Emperor Qin Shi Huangdi arranged to be accompanied in his tomb by eight thousand terra cotta soldiers.

Not to be outdone by the annals of history, the mortal remains of Maximillian von Lichtenbichler, First King of Zarenga Chi, were dropped from a hydrogen balloon into a volcano, the potentate forever entombed in the magma of the sacred mountain.

As such, a tradition had been established, and his successor Maximillian II was likewise dropped from on high into molten rock.

Of course, as luck would have it, the person who cut the rope on the dangling shrouded corpse was none other than the King's heir.

Which of course meant that it befell me to be the

one to go aloft with an aeronaut and dispatch Max III into Mumu's maw.

I had only been in a hot air balloon once before in New Mexico. I was fishing the San Juan River, and there was a balloon rally nearby. One evening at the bar I was cajoled by a comely vixen to join her on a flight the following day. My fear of heights is a somewhat recent development due to my trials in the Caribbean and then in a hang glider in Kazakhstan, so at the time I found the ride enjoyable enough, even if the flight included her boyfriend. Not once did I feel the flight was unsafe, and we glided peacefully if a little frigidly over desert terrain on a bright blue morning.

That flight, however, was over canyons and valleys, not over an active volcano. I was bound by my word that I would participate in the funeral, and so I buckled down and determined that I could endure this if that's what it took to avoid becoming His Majesty Boone the First. At the very least I would have bragging rights for a lifetime as I was quite certain that I would never encounter another soul who had attained such a feat.

Not that Terry Orbach, my intrepid weevil-like publicist, would let anybody ever forget it. It had been three days since I caught the striped marlin and had my interlude with Foresh, so the notion that I would have had time to fish for wahoo with Ando seemed laughable. In that time, by hook and by crook, Terry had insinuated himself with Amalgamated Consumables. His mission was to document the state funeral and all the backstage preparation – it was to be part documentary, part a 'launch' promotional package of yours truly for the African beverage market. And so he had shown up in khaki's and a pith helmet all set for safari, or one would have supposed, camera crew in tow. Terry was back in true form, the crew zooming in on my every waking moment and even the most mundane task or action subject to another 'take.'

Boone, don't rub your nose, it looks like you're picking your nostril. We'll have to do another take of that sip of coffee.

And it wasn't just the indomitable Orbach following my every move but a squad of Amalgamated's publicists who were clearly upset that Terry had been dropped in their midst, and they second-guessed Terry's every directorial decision. They would push up on their glasses, share a glance, and then one of them would step next to him and say: "Are you sure this is sending the right message?"

Arguments erupted, phone calls to Kinkaid were placed, and then Terry and the other publicists would have to have a pow-wow or some such with a mediator – which usually gave me my only snippet of peace while awake or not in the bathroom.

Preparations for the funeral included tailors fitting me for a white dress uniform, cut just so at the nape to best frame my Cross of Valor. They also fit me for a tuxedo for the honors dinner the night before the actual balloon funeral and a dark suit for the wake the day after. My hair and mustache were trimmed just so, my cuticles daintied, and my face facialed. And there was a fair amount of plucking stray hairs from every nook and cranny, from my nose to the hairs on my chest.

Rehearsals were required for every aspect of the honors dinner, reception lines, and even the catering for the wake.

I had to meet with dignitaries arriving from other nations wanting to extend their condolences and try to ingratiate themselves with the man they assumed would be King. Likewise, I had to meet with members of the foreign press to say a few words, Terry forever poking me at every utterance he thought misconceived.

All the while, Tanya was nowhere to be seen, and I had received a note on my refrigerator that simply said *Sorry – T.* Well, I assumed it was from Tanya. If for no other reason than it was part of a pattern, of sorts. Foresh lit out early the next morning after our tryst, and I found a note *from her* that simply said: *For my country – XOForesh.*

I mean, what the devil was that all about?

Anyway, the endurance test continued when I was fit for a ceremonial sword to go with my white uniform, which is more involved than you might think. If the scabbard is too long or heavy you will trip over it; too short and light and it will swing between your legs and trip you up (quite painfully, I might add.) The scabbard has to be positioned on the hip so it does not spank you as you walk, or turn into a pendulum. Ultimately, I had to learn to walk differently to keep the blasted thing hanging straight down or move politely with my leg.

There were flash cards of all the corporate big-wigs that I needed to memorize, and their wives. Royal protocols were dispensed, and then there were photo sessions, to include those of me in my uniform and cross standing nobly in front of a large oil portrait of Maximillian I.

That portrait was a bit unnerving, by the way. The Original Max, my great grandfather, bore no little resemblance to yours truly, with a magnificent set of whiskers and white uniform, eyebrow cocked, and gaze set on the distant future when his drunkard great grandson would shirk his duty. Next to him was a ylang-ylang tree, the droopy yellow flowers in profusion. Behind him were the distant palm-treed hills and Mumu, a balloon floating nearby. *How prescient.*

So by the time the big day arrived, I was quite ready to put all this behind me.

Not to mention Terry. He was on overdrive. What in the world had I been thinking by inviting him down to Zarenga Chi? Ah, yes, the thumb drive. Well, likely as not Foresh was in New York handing over her copy of the drive to a drinking buddy of mine at the New York Times. So charging Terry with the task was a redundancy and possibly unnecessary. Yet it was too important to leave up to just one person, I supposed. I just hadn't got around to it yet.

After all that prep, it was with relief rather than dread that I stood before the basket of the black funerary balloon. The launch was in the late afternoon because balloons behave more reliably in cooler daytime temperatures. I stood on a raised stage surrounded by dignitaries in tuxedoes. In front of me were many thousands of Zarengi in a vast park. The men all wore ties and the ladies all wore dresses. Those assembled sang the national anthem in German, an oompah number, tubas farting rhythmically.

You would have thought me an extra from the back lot at Universal what with my hilted sword and scabbard, white gloves folded into my black gun belt, stiff white pants and tunic, red cross of valor around my neck and white German pith helmet on my head.

Marching carefully forward so that my sword did not sway uncontrollably, I stopped briefly to place my hand on the flag-cocooned remains of Max III tethered to the side of the balloon. It was when I stopped at the side of the balloon basket that I realized there was one thing I had not practiced: climbing into a balloon basket wearing a scabbard. So I clasped the scabbard to my leg and hopped my behind on the edge. I swung my legs in, avoiding a most embarrassing pratfall in the process. I dare say anyone watching would have thought I'd done this maneuver many times, perhaps with the Bavarian Balloon Detachment.

The Caucasian aeronaut wore goggles and a black jumpsuit. He was a slight man, and he bowed his head slightly, the voluminous black balloon hanging above. With a clipped accent, he said under his breath: "Step back next to me. His Highness is very heavy, and when we ascend the basket will tip away from us unless we balance by standing at the other side, of course."

I stepped back, and the aeronaut nodded at the balloon crew around us, who loosened the ropes.

We began to ascend.

Striking a pose that I imagined mirrored that of Max I's portrait, I caught sight of Terry and the film crew in the front row below the stage. My publicist was frantically saluting.

Ah, yes, the salute. He had made me practice the proper salute for my lift off, and I, of course had forgotten it, lost in thought about when I might have a shot at a wahoo, or at the very least, smother myself in an avalanche of cocktails.

As such, I muffed it, pounding a fist to my chest and then extending my arm out and palm downward. Where I came up with that I had no idea. Was that not the ancient Roman salute, *Hail Cesar?* I certainly hoped it didn't look like a Nazi salute.

Terry all but curled up into a ball on the ground with dismay at my gaff.

Rather amusing when I think on it afterward, and likely the bungled salute was a subliminal pushback at my obsessive handler.

Flames leapt from the propane burner as the aeronaut quickened our ascent, the audience below singing and crying and swaying, Max III's bulk dangling ten feet below one corner of the basket.

Alrighty, Mr. Boone. Let's get this over with. Then it's the wake, where we might carve out a slice of prime imbibing time.

I looked down at the security people but still couldn't see Tanya, which concerned me. Then my eyes landed on Linus Trimble, his girth and wild mane of white hair. He gave me a small two finger salute from his temple, his Cheshire smile knowing something I didn't, as ever.

Up we rose, like an elevator in a skyscraper, the crowd's song echoing, and they began not to look like individual people but more like a nubby, multicolored carpet. The park below with its soccer fields, gazebos and swimming pool began to look like a toy train set without the trains.

The balloon shifted horizontally as we ascended into a breeze blowing toward the volcano, which began to look more ominous at that height because it was black and massive.

The aeronaut continued to blast flame into the balloon, which towered above us.

Then all at once, the aeronaut switched off the burners, the pilot light small and flickering. The silence, as it were, was deafening, and the cool air was becoming cold.

"Have you floated over the volcano before?" I asked, peering down at the aeronaut next to me.

He simply nodded, looking away up at little ribbons on the tethers to see which way the wind was going, and eyeing the altimeter and thermometer on the propane console at the center of the basket. Not much of a conversationalist, and he did not meet my eye. On our side of the balloon I noted that there were sand bags over the side to help compensate for Max's heft, and perhaps the balloonist's lack of heft.

Like Zeus clearing his throat, Mumu emitted a stuttering thrum that rattled my innermost bones, and I could smell the sulfur from the fumes even at that distance.

We continued to ascend, and as we approached the height of the mountain's peak, the wind picked up, and we began to drift faster toward the forbidding mountain cauldron. The carpet of palms and forest began to surrender to rocky terrain dotted by shrubs. My hands were getting cold and I tucked them under my armpits.

On a technical note, hot air balloons rise best in lower temperatures. Conversely, once over the heat emitted from the volcano, we would automatically begin to descend, so it was up to the aeronaut to make sure that we did not descend too quickly and end up cinders ourselves.

So I asked the pilot anxiously: "How low over the crater will we go?"

"Of course, we will become low, you cut rope, and then we rise fast without the fat man, catch the wind and then land on the beach far side."

I noticed that my aeronaut friend had a harness and was clipped to the side of the basket, and I pointed at it. "Should I be clipped on, too?"

He scrunched his mouth and shook his head.

The sooty black rim of the crater passed a few hundred feet below and immediately we felt the warm air and began to descend. At first I could not see the lava for the swirling clouds of sulfurous steam, but then it cleared and I could see ulcerous red patches of flame in a black mass, cracks neon red in the molten crust.

I coughed from the steam and held out my utility knife. "Now?"

He held up a hand, and the rim grew near. Out of the wind, we sailed more slowly and directly over a lake of fire – surely a dead ringer for Hades lair itself.

My pilot held out a hand. "You may proceed, of course."

Oh of course, time to drop a dead man into a lava lake, of course.

With all due dispatch I stepped forward, the balloon tipping in that direction as I did so.

Looking directly down at the dangling, flag-shrouded remains of Max and the pit of scorching damnation beyond, I went to work straight away on the suspending rope, eager to rid ourselves of this ballast and begin to rise away from the furnace.

The basket lurched violently.

I pitched forward, dropping the knife.

Below I saw the sand bags splash down into the blistering crust, glowing red lava sloshing lazily from the penetrations.

The pilot had intentionally cut loose the counterweights just as we were pitched over and I was leaning out!

I lost my grip on the railing, and fumbled for the basket frame.

My body twisted, my legs swinging as I was headed head over heels for a fall from the basket.

Then I felt my belt tug tight – my scabbard had caught in the weave of the basket. I was pinned in place at my belt.

Yet my legs spun out over the edge of the basket, out over the searing crater of doom, that ceremonial sword and the fiber of the basket the only thing keeping me from dropping over the side and joining Max in the fiery depths of Vulcan's forge.

I kicked furiously like riding a bicycle and spun my legs full circle and back into the basket.

My vision blurred with panic: my pilot had unclipped himself and lunged at my feet, trying to push them and me back over the edge.

Now the entire basket was practically sideways with all the weight on one side and we were dropping faster, the heat becoming intense.

Max had to be cut loose so we would rise and not splash down in the lava.

Significant weight had to go over the side, pronto.

His face red and cursing, the pilot grabbed my foot and began to shove, as I shoved back.

Until suddenly, I didn't.

I pulled when he shoved, kicking my legs to the side.

He landed on my chest.

If I couldn't cut Max loose, let the aeronaut go over and stop our descent.

I planted my feet thrust my pelvis upward with everything I had.

His knees raked up my chest; his boots kicked my jaw as he slid over me.

Then he was gone.

I only heard a muffled shout and hissing plop from below.

The balloon stopped descending, but seemed to waffle, uncertain whether it might decide to rise again.

The basket came more upright but was still heavily tilted.

Struggling with my scabbard, it seemed to take forever to free it, and I recall thinking: *And I thought I'd been in a hot spot before!*

Jerking the scabbard free, I crouched, fumbled and drew the sword, the blade singing over the pop and hiss of the lava.

Looking over the edge of the basket at Max, I saw that we were not fifty feet from the molten red rock, the heat growing immense. Max's shroud was smoldering as I hacked furiously with the sword at the rope.

Being a ceremonial sword, it was not exactly sharp, and I had to flail like a lunatic at the fraying rope to finally make it part – just as Max's shroud burst into flame.

He plunged noiselessly into the burning lake.

The basket bobbed back upright, but we were still going down slowly even without Max – the growing heat rising from the lava was neutralizing the buoyancy of the hot air of the balloon.

I jumped to my feet and wrenched the knob on the burners, a huge tongue of flame shooting up into the balloon.

Go! Please dear God, go up.

That little two fingered salute from Trimble? Something told me that was not just a farewell but a goodbye. *He knew.*

Ah, but I knew something he didn't, namely that I had tossed that infernal (literally) pilot overboard and escaped. But had I?

I couldn't see the walls of the crater, just steam.

There was a loud jet of gas from below; it smelled of burnt flesh and charred bone.

Mumu burped.

The propane blaze above me roared heat into the black balloon. When I peered up at its shadowy shape in the swirling sulfurous steam, it hovered above me like either an oppressing angel of death or the gigantic winged Garuda of deliverance snatching me from the brink of doom.

Then all at once the steam cleared.

The rim!

I was going up!

Slowly.

Cooler air filled my lungs, and I looked down to see the flickers of neon red below receding into the mist.

Up! Up!

I tried to crank the burner knob higher but it was as high as it would go.

As the balloon emerged from the crater and hit much cooler air it became like an express elevator, accelerating quickly and then rising steadily.

The valley below spilled out before me, the crowd and stage visible far below and in the distance.

I rose into a stream of air that pushed the balloon away from Mumu, away from the launch site, and toward the far side of the island where a large spit of sand pointed out to the blue horizon, the sun setting off to my left.

I was so relieved that tears cascaded down my cheeks and into my whiskers. I laughed at the feeble fates that had tried to undo me.

Then, all at once, I realized, that I had to land the balloon down on that distant spit of sand where the recovery vehicles were tiny dots.

So I turned off the burner.

Yet as I rose into cooler air, the hot air in the balloon became even more buoyant.

Even with the burner off the balloon continued to rise, higher and higher.

And the higher I went, the windier it was.

Had I been an actual balloonist, I would have known that there was a relief valve in the top of the balloon to expel an excess of hot air and descend. However, the lever that was connected to that vent was not labeled, and when you are thousands of feet in the air in a balloon, the last thing you do is start pulling unmarked levers. Not that I even noticed the lever at the time. All I knew how to do was turn the burner up and turn it down. All those years ago in New Mexico I failed to take proper note of how the balloon worked.

Panic resumed as I realized that I was going to overshoot the spit of sand, the recovery vehicles below tiny specs.

Panic doubled when I realized I was in a balloon I had no idea how to operate, had no way to steer – a balloon that was black and racing out to sea as night was falling, no land in sight.

How could anybody rescue me?

I would have to ditch in the ocean to be saved by helicopter or sea plane.

Could they even find me at night? Or would they risk running into a black balloon at night? Presumably radar would prevent that? Do balloons show up on radar? How do I land softly in the ocean and not have the basket flip over on top of me?

Wait. These rescuers would be the same people who covered up the fact that the assassins were Russian, and likely the same people who just tried to have me thrown into a bottomless pit of magma. So exactly why would they now try to come rescue me?

They wouldn't.

The spit of sand receded into the distance behind me, darkness descending, and the western horizon ahead of me a golden red line.

The prospect of yours truly, in the middle of the dark ocean, floundering, with no rescue coming, was a nightmare. Would the gondola float?

I was getting cold, and made chillier when I thought of...*sharks*. Floundering with sharks.

Escape?

I had only dodged one specter of doom for another.

Cold, alone and dark, I sailed silently out to sea.

CHAPTER 16

LAND HO!

No sweeter words ever passed my lips.

I wasn't sure at first light, but the small smudge on the horizon grew.

Praise Poseidon that this apparition had not manifested itself in the dark or I might have missed the island.

As you might well imagine, I had spent a harrowing, sleepless night of self-reproach, simmering vengeance, and outright terror at the prospect of running out of propane and descending slowly into a splash-down into what I imagined a shark infested sea. At night.

And what a night. The sky was gushing with stars, a sliver of moon to one side. And utter silence. I felt as if I was in outer space. Never have I seen such a dark and sparkling nocturnal display – too bad I was not in any mood to enjoy it. Quite the contrary.

I reflected on the relative cakewalk I had experienced mere months before when I was stranded in the Russian

Far East boreal forests.

At least I was on land, with fly rods, and with a modicum of liquor. I had not thought to bring a flask, and if I had, the shape would likely have shown through my white military tunic.

I fairly prayed.

If anybody is listening, please let me die on land or at least with a cocktail or fishing rod in hand.

Of course, I had not spent the night merely cowering and blubbering about my predicament, though I would have preferred to do so. The night's task at hand was figuring out how to control the elevation of the balloon. As one would imagine, allowing the air in the envelope above to cool caused me to descend. Heating it caused me to rise. The trick of course how much of either? Likewise, I found that if I sank lower I went slower – it was windier and colder higher. And I did not necessarily want to go slowly, I wanted to get to land as fast as possible, so I shivered and sailed onward.

Enacting a few practice runs, I found that using by only short bursts of flame I could maintain a certain height, so I began to perform countdowns to see how far and how fast I would sink depending on the number of flame bursts I employed. As such, I was able to affect a steady slow descent, though admittedly I never came anywhere near the surface of the ominous waters chockablock with imagined sharks.

Therefore, to make a landing on the island ahead, I had to try to approximate distance, altitude and descent rates. The altimeter was a useful aid, but the calculus was not exactly slide rule science.

Heart pounding, my impulse was to hedge my bets and try to land short of the island, even in the water, and then swim to shore. Bound and determined: do not overshoot what was likely to be my last chance at survival. Or at the very least, my last chance to die on land unmolested by sea creatures with great gnashing teeth. My propane tanks were almost empty.

Ironic, isn't it, that an angler should be so afraid of becoming bait?

Descending to five hundred feet, the balloon slowed as I made my final approach, the sun rising behind me.

Look at the sand and the trees! Fresh water, will there be water?

What lay ahead across the shrinking expanse of bright blue was likely less than a square mile in size, with a rocky, forested mound in the center topped in forest. Palms backed the beach, and I could see coconuts hanging from under the fronds. If nothing else I could drink that.

I saw no signs of habitation, but oh, what if there were? I said another short non-committal prayer.

I began to collect what I could from the basket that I might need to survive. I had the sword, of course, and I removed the scabbard from my belt so that in a crash it wouldn't trip me up. There was a first aid kit, a spark ignitor for the propane burner, a fire extinguisher and a length of rope that was the tail end of what supported

Max. There was also a small cylinder of oxygen and a mask – I imagined this was for any one aboard who became lightheaded from the altitude. I secured my pith helmet with the chin strap, anticipating a possible crash landing.

On a chain around my neck was the cylinder containing the silver thumb drive and in my front pocket was my wallet with I think seventy dollars in U.S. mintage and assorted credit cards. I had not brought my cell phone, but I did have my Zarenga Chi and U.S. passports. Whenever I am abroad, I always keep my passports with me so they aren't stolen or go missing, stranding me. A little OCD, I know.

Of course I hoped to salvage the balloon basket and balloon, both of which could be used to make a shelter if need be. So I really wanted to land on the beach.

Rising sun warming my back, the balloon inexplicably began to rise as I approached the beach.

Blast! The sun is heating the air in the balloon!

Fifty feet over the sand, I was headed directly for the rocky, forested outcrop.

I was tempted to jump, but the likelihood of breaking an ankle was good, and that would be my death knell if this island were uninhabited.

Crashing into the rocks was likewise perilous.

I shouted a vile oath that echoed off the rocks ahead.

A short blast of flame rose me up to the level of the forested mound, but not entirely above it.

The bottom of the basket crashed into the canopy,

dragging through branches, yet I could see the other side of the island, and I hoped this drag might have the unintended consequence of helping me land on the beach ahead.

Oh, there was an unintended consequence, but not what I imagined.

Bats.

The trees were filled with roosting bats.

Now, when I say bats, you of course imagine the evil little flying voles that fit in your hand, yes?

Alas, these were another variety altogether. I had seen them on nature shows but never in person, much less in a startled colony that erupted from the forest.

These were flying foxes, so called because they are enormous and the size of a small fox with a wing span of I'd say five feet.

Dropped to the bottom of the basket, I struggled to pull my sword to swat at the frenzied flying vixens that shrieked and smacked into the balloon, suspender frame and basket all around me. Black wings meshed in a dark kaleidoscope above me, and I expected one to fall into the basket with me at any second.

An onslaught of giant angry bats: just what I needed at that juncture. As if my overnight voyage had not been harrowing enough, and then the landing attempt, now frenzied bats!

Yet no sooner had the onslaught begun it stopped, bat squeals disappearing away into the forest. I leapt to my feet, giving the balloon a short shot of flame to make sure I made it to the beach and did not crash in the forest.

The damn sun kept beating down on the balloon – and because the balloon was black it was absorbing heat rapidly. My entire night of descent experiments was out the window, and the balloon rose, passing the tree line and over the beach at about a hundred feet up.

My eyes fixed on that mystery lever, the one I had not noticed way back at Zarenga Chi but had since took to wondering what it did.

As they say, no time like the present. Or as my father would have said when a glass of milk was spilled: *Pickles find their way into your sandwich whether you like it or not.*

Laughter and tears accompanied a quick descent and abrupt thud onto the middle of the wide beach, the basket falling sideways and me tumbling out like dice from a cup.

The big black bag of balloon withered slowly to the sand, and partially draped over the basket.

Just the sound of the waves crashing on shore, and the stray croak of a frigate bird.

I lay on my back, sun warming the tears on my cheeks as I wept, the firmness of terra firma on my back more welcome than any cocktail, fish or caress.

Smoke?

That's when I realized the balloon had caught fire.

CHAPTER 17

UNINHABITED. MAROONED.

I walked the perimeter of the island and the only sign of human habitation was a stone fire ring and some trash washed up on the beach. Both were my first and most important discoveries on Toad Caye. Yes, I'd already named it, because of what the forested mound in the center looked like. It was steep on the west side, with a jungled shelf for a snout, rocky outcrop atop the head, then a gently sloping forest that devolved into mangroves at the east where the legs would be. The shore was sandy west and south, and the north shore was rockier with tidal pools. A reef surrounded all but the west side.

When I say important, it means that once I had established I was alone, I had to shift into survival mode. And the garbage meant that some form of civilization might not be so far away. It also meant some plastic bottles, and a detergent bottle, all of which I collected eagerly.

My second most important discovery would be

water. Bats lived on Toad Caye, so there must be water and possibly fruit.

Returning back to the partially burnt remains of the balloon, I surveyed the damage. I managed to pull the flaming nylon away from the tipped basket and the pilot light that had set it alight. Throwing sand, I managed to save half of the balloon, which would likely be sufficient to make a tent and more. It was enormous.

First things first. With my sword, I marched toward the forest line and coconut palms.

Opening coconuts may sound like a formidable task, and it would be if not for the fact that I was an advanced cocktailer who has fished tropical locations. Fresh coconut milk, or better still, a cocktail made in a fresh nut, is a treat of the first order.

I had not, however, been the one to climb the tree to get the nut. Obviously I picked the tree that leaned the most and was lower to the ground than the others.

Removing my stiff uniform tunic was be essential, as was removal of my shoes. Decked out only in my white uniform pants, it took me a half hour or so of trial and error before I successfully mimicked the native peoples I had seen climb coconut trees. Seven husked nuts dropped to the ground, which I hoped would hold me until I could find a better source of water and food, assuming there was one.

So you know for your next stint as a castaway:

1. Remove the outer shuck by pounding the pointy end on a rock. This will split the husk and then

you can wrench it apart. A ceremonial sword helps but is not necessary.

2.   Once the bare nut is in hand, you will observe that it is slightly oblong, and therefore has two ends. One end, the North Pole, has three brown dots that look vaguely like two eyes and a mouth – the eyes being smaller than the mouth. Run an imaginary line from between the two eyes at the North Pole to where it bisects the nut's Equator. This is the sweet spot. Holding the nut so that its axis is tilted forward forty-five degrees, smack the sweet spot on a hard edge (granite counter top, nearby rock, etc.) It is rather amazing how neatly a crack will form around the nut's equator. You may have to strike it several times before it halves completely, but you must do so carefully so as to retain as much coconut milk as possible.

I sat on a volcanic rock in the shade at the edge of the forest and base of a small viny cliff, surveying the beach, the remains of my balloon and the deep blue horizon beyond. I used my ceremonial sword to pry out morsels of coconut.

How utterly ironic.

How much like and not like being stranded in the woods and wilderness of Russia's Far East. At least in a forest on a continent I could walk my way out overland, and there was plenty of fresh water and little trout to gnaw on.

As there, Toad Caye would pose challenges if I were to survive for long without rescue. The fire ring I had seen told me someone occasionally came to the island and stayed the night. The ground was littered with empty boxes of ammunition printed with Cyrillic letters. That did not give me much confidence that the last people to enjoy a fire at Toad Caye would provide deliverance. It is no secret that the sea in the vicinity of Somalia and as far out as the Seychelles is scattered with pirates. While the pirate scourge is in decline, they are still out there.

I had a number of things going for me.

One: I was healthy and strong, and had better make sure I stayed that way and above all did not injure myself. The little first aid kit in the balloon would suffice were I to cut a finger but would be useless if I broke my arm or leg.

Two: it is well established that I am not wed to fine dining. That is, I am not someone who requires regular nutrition. I can fish all day and not eat until dinner, while some of my compatriots might need to munch on candy bars and snacks to get them through. So I can go for periods of time without much food and not be the worse for it. Yet to address item one, I would of course need to find something to eat other than coconuts.

Three: My father, as a professor of American frontier history, emulated his heroes like my namesake by insisting that our family eat game meat regularly. That being the case, I was familiar with how to clean and dress animals for roasting. Unfortunately, it was patently clear that the only game I was likely to find was the bats or possibly rats. Assuming I could catch one without getting bitten and coming down with some horrendous infection. My strong suit would be whatever I could scavenge from the sea, of course, but without my fly rods, I would be relegated to whatever morsels I might find in tide pools.

Four: The balloon's wreckage. The propane igniter – the same type used for starting welding torches – did not require fuel and was more or less flint and steel that would provide me with fire for a long time. There wasn't much propane left in the tanks but that could prove useful as well. The nylon of the inflatable part would provide a tent or tarpaulin, and also a membrane to collect rain water, directing it into whatever plastic bottles I could find on the beach. The basket – made of what seemed wicker around a metal frame – might be part of a shelter, or it might provide useful materials like wire, string and rope once unraveled.

Squinting at the blue horizon on that cloudless day, the waves crashing mildly on the beach, I tried to imagine my permanent vacation once I wriggled out of my contract with Amalgamated Consumables. I'd have a dock, and a little skiff, and a simple thatched bar down the road where I could go sip rum and swill beer and talk about nothing with the friendly bartender, flirt with the girls. Would that ever happen – now? Or was this my ultimate fate? Was this my permanent vacation?

The gods mocked me: all I wanted to do was get away from the hoi polloi, from the camera flashes and promotional events and expectations and just be by myself, at least for a while, and have no one come and try to use me for some uncertain end.

Careful what you wish for.

You can't go through what I had over the last couple years and remain sane without some time to reflect on what happened. Killing people, seeing others killed, explosions and all manner of mayhem – did that have any significance or add greater context to my life?

Or was it was just something to be endured and move on from, leaving those experiences in the past like an apple core tossed to the side of the trail, detritus in my wake.

Were this my last stand, I had better make the best of it and find water, make shelter, figure out that whole food thing.

And somehow be ready for the possibility of pirates.

CHAPTER 18

TWO WEEKS LATER I WAS STILL ALIVE.

More to the point, it looked as if I might remain that way indefinitely barring a catastrophe: I had found fresh water.

A little sulfurous, but technically fresh. I had found a hot spring trickling out of the rock face on a large shelf of the western face of the rocky mound – in effect, on the toad's snout. I guessed that Toad Caye may have been created by some sort of volcanic vent. Collection of this steady dribble was accomplished by creating a depression in the dirt below the dribble and lining it with nylon. From the ponded water I could fill the plastic bottles.

After a few nights on the edge of the forest and beach, it occurred to me that a more permanent camp should be established in a more secure vantage, both to conceal my location and to provide a longer view of my surroundings. And why not on that promontory – the snout – where the water was? Trees formed a bat-free canopy that provided relief from the heat, and I was able to use part of the nylon balloon to install a tarpaulin sub-roof, the corners fastened to trees with nylon twine that I harvested from the wicker basket. I cleared the ground, which was a thin layer of soil atop rock, and likewise covered it in black balloon nylon tarp.

I cut a hole in the tarp floor for a fire ring, made from rocks. Dried coconut husks, once ignited, made perfect coals for cooking. There was little viable firewood on the island. The forest floor was damp and fallen wood rotted. Occasional driftwood sufficed.

I fashioned a bed out of large leaves on the ground covered by more black nylon.

The sides I left open to get the breeze and keep smoke moving out, and with my ceremonial sword I hacked away many of the vines and branches so I had a dandy westward view. While I supposed that a boat could approach from any direction, I knew the African continent was west of me, with Madagascar to the southwest.

From below on the beach, my perch and black tarpaulin were barely noticeable, which was the way I wanted it.

My hope was that some sort of commercial boat would come close enough that I might use the propane tanks and burner to signal them. I had mounted the tanks and burners in the rocks behind and above my camp, atop the toad's head. From the highest point, the flames would be high enough that a boat could not miss it.

I saw aircraft regularly to the northwest. They twinkled and moved silently, often leaving a contrail, probably at thirty-five thousand feet. No way to signal them for help.

Food. Other than coconuts, I had found some of those peachy, orangey mystery fruits growing wild in bushes all over the island. I decided they needed a name and so I called them boogles. They were much more bitter than the cultivated variety, yet I became accustomed to them. My guess was that the flying foxes did not eat them for this reason, yet the rest of any fruit that may have grown on the island they had decimated.

Likewise, I found that the bats liked coconut. This I discovered when I found one picking at the remains of one I'd eaten. As the bats were unable to open coconuts themselves, this meant the local crop was all mine.

So I had boogles and coconuts as a starter.

I'd discovered a bush with small white berries, yet I knew from my father's frontier know-how that white berries are almost always poisonous. This gave me an idea. Perhaps I could lace an open coconut with the berries and poison one of the bats. They roosted high in the trees and there was little chance of me getting one with my sword or throwing rocks.

Ah, yes, the sword – I set about putting an edge on it using local rocks.

Most evenings the bats flew west and out of sight, returning in the early morning. I surmised that they fed at night on some other island or the mainland, indicating that either one could not be that far away. This heartened me beyond mere hope to near certainty that it would not be overly long before I was rescued.

As such, I elected not to poison any bats and forgo what was likely an unappealing culinary episode.

Yet I could not rest in my search for other food, and seafood seemed a logical target.

I found a small octopus in the rocks on the east shore, and cooked it over an open flame. It was vile, yet I swallowed the nourishment just the same.

More appetizing were some conchs, their shells with long spikes splayed out like an open hand. I knew from trips to the Bahamas how to extract the slug inside by cutting a hole near the peak of the shell and inserting the tip of the sword to cut the animal free of its home. While unappetizing in its natural state, I have a great fondness for the taste of these slugs, and they were excellent soaked in boogle juice and roasted over the coconut husk coals.

Fish eluded me without the benefit of my tackle. I had made a spear by lashing my red cross of valor to a length of bamboo but could not get close enough to try to spear them.

There was not a lot of bamboo on the island and I did not want to deplete it in case I needed to build something, but I did cut a long thin stalk and was in the process of using threads from nylon string to wrap the stalk at intervals for strength. I kept it in the sun to dry it, and began likewise to make fishing line from the nylon string. Steel staples from the basket were to be made into hooks. I did not take this endeavor very seriously as I was sure to be discovered before many more weeks.

I determined to stick to foraging and forgo hunting and fishing.

Besides, my labors were better spent seeing if I could make a libation from boogles. I squeezed a dozen into the detergent bottle and sealed it. With the tubing from the oxygen mask, I fashioned a relief valve by capturing water in a loop. For fermentation to occur, it is essential that the juice be deprived of air yet allow carbon dioxide to escape the container.

Sitting by the glowing coals as the sun set, I would sip my bitter sulfur water laced with tangy, sour boogle and wonder what was going on back in Zarenga Chi. Possibly the 'authorities' claimed I had died in the volcano, yet the balloon recovery crew would have seen me float away. Perhaps they said they searched and could not find me, or that they found the balloon and basket floating in the ocean, the heir to the throne presumed drowned and eaten by sharks?

They got what they wanted – it was either me as their pliant king accomplice or an end to royalty all together.

Yet the notes from Tanya and Foresh confounded me. They knew something I didn't, and had assumed that I would discover what they meant had I not drifted off into the sunset.

Tanya's "Sorry" – did she regret getting involved in 'handling' me or not being intimate in some way or had she done something I did not know about? What could that have been?

And Foresh's "For my country" – usually that is said in conjunction with "I did it for." Was her visit for her country? That indicated she needed to justify something she did as a perceived patriotic duty.

Even though it was quite warm, I got a chill, darkness settling in and the stars freckling the navy sky.

Did the two notes have any connection? Quite the coincidence getting two notes like that at more or less the same time.

Was Foresh…had Foresh decided not to deliver the drive? She didn't know what was on it, I simply said it was photos for a friend. Did someone ask her not to deliver it and instead divert it? Hand it over to Kinkaid or…Trimble? Or Tanya?

In hindsight, it seemed a little odd that Foresh would risk swimming under my dock to come see me. Did someone purposely put her up to doing so just to get the drive? Did the security detail let her pass, on instructions?

Had she been assigned to seduce me from the beginning, as Tanya suggested?

There were listening devices in my townhouse, they heard Max say he had damning information on 'this thumb drive.' Maybe when they were cleaning up the explosion and carefully collecting all those little piles of debris they were looking for the thumb drive. And when they couldn't find it, suspected I had it.

My jaw tightened as I realized that Tanya – who knew of Foresh – may have put her up to getting the thumb drive from me. Well, who the hell knew, maybe it was Trimble. Or Kinkaid. Or Putin's people.

That's why she was sorry.

Betrayal? Well, I did not own up to having the drive, and it was the information Tanya had been sent to have me collect. So I was holding out on her. Perhaps *she* felt a little betrayed.

The other drives? I never got a chance to give one to Terry. I could only assume that my townhouse had been thoroughly picked over and the other thumb drives discovered and summarily destroyed.

The one around my neck was likely the only one left.

Sitting alone with the glowing red coals and sparkling endless sky, gloom gripped me knowing that there could be no trust between me and Tanya. In my heart of hearts I had held out hope for the two of us. She as much as said that her 'job' took priority. Should I be surprised?

Strange that this realization about the notes came only then. Perhaps my subconscious mind had been mulling it over in private before revealing the results of its investigation.

I had been played by two women close to me – that was about as bitter a pill as my boogle sulfur wine.

What was my future going forward, should I manage to survive being marooned and be rescued? Not as before. As king? As a permanent vacationer? As a has-been?

Survival and rescue would be a second chance at life, and opportunity. It was the chance to become the man I wanted to be not the man others wanted me to be.

I gently shook the metal cylinder, listening to the silver drive rattle inside.

It was the sound of resolve.

This isn't over yet.

CHAPTER 19

IT WAS A **WEDNESDAY.**

I'd lost count of the weeks and days, but knew that I had seen at least five full moons. I suppose some would have cut hash marks into a tree or scraped a rock to count the days. For me, that would have only made a somewhat desperate situation worse and driven me to despair. Under these circumstances, you have to forget about rescue and focus on your survival infrastructure as though deliverance is never coming. Had I not done so, I surely would have perished, or gone insane, or both.

Likewise, the prospect of fashioning some sort of sea-faring craft and setting sail to the west was patently absurd. Yes, I had plenty of black nylon balloon material to make a sail, and no doubt could have fashioned something that would float. There was an opening in the reef that I could easily have passed through. But leaving terra firma for the shark-infested swells of the open ocean, at the mercy of the wind and storms and men in boats with guns? Not even a consideration.

Complicating my predicament was twice witnessing speed boats passing beyond the reef. In these boats were slender black men holding assault rifles, the kind with ammunition magazines that curve forward, similar to the types I had seen the Chinese military carry. The men were not in uniform. Pirates.

One day they would land on Toad Caye, and I had to be prepared for it.

In that regard, it was a good idea to keep the beach clean of any indication that I was present. My first order of business upon their arrival would be to keep my head low and wait until they left. I managed to roll the balloon basket into the forest edge next to my path so that it was no longer on the beach. Then I realized the wicker blended well with the forest and would make a dandy duck blind, of a sort. OK, a pirate blind. I cut a slot in the wicker through which I could observe the western vista of beach and topaz sea. Then I piled rocks up against it as fortification against bullets.

My second order of business was to install some level of fortification to prevent them from approaching my lair. I found a use for empty conch shells and their long points by burying them in the leaf litter on the embankment up to my camp on the ledge. I still ate a lot of conch because they were easy to collect in the grassy shallows on the lea side of the island. Hundreds had been consumed and now formed a hidden barrier and stumbling block to any approach except by the main path that I used for egress.

I also installed them in the forest at the toad's back, where the bats roosted, along with vines to act as tripping hazards.

The path to my lair, of course, would be an immediate tip-off that someone was living in the forest. So I kept the entry point from the beach covered in leaf litter. Still, I had to assume that they might venture further in the forest and stumble upon the path. So I camouflaged my path and created a false path that branched from it. This false path led to a sinkhole in the rocks – when it rained, water cascaded down the rock face there and washed the soil away into some sort of void deep in the ground. At the bottom was a jagged opening in the rock no bigger than a keg. This seemed an ideal spot for a tiger trap.

With one side of the balloon basket I crafted a base for an array of sharpened sticks and bamboo shoots that I lowered into the pit like a coffin into a grave. I was not going to risk trying to climb down into it as the soil on the sides was very soft and sandy – I feared not being able to climb out. The platform of spikes spanned the washout hole in the bottom, and a lattice of branches, vine and leaf litter created the illusion that there was no sink hole. I even tossed sand and gravel onto the false ground to create the illusion of a path across it. At the rock face next to it, I had to leave a hole for the rainwater to pass under my false floor, but I did not think it was particularly noticeable.

On the chance that anybody managed to find the

true path, I had installed booby traps comprised of cocked tree branches set by trigger wires to wallop interlopers.

What all these defenses meant was that I had a very intricate commute each day down to the beach, hopping in a zigzag from one safe spot to the next.

Heavy rains would set off the trip wires and so these defenses were hardly maintenance free.

The third 'order of business?' Offense, of which I had little that could match even simple military weaponry. There was my ceremonial sword, of course, which would be the last defense. And I had my spear tipped with my sharpened Cross of Valor – also of limited use against humans but not so bad at spearing nurse sharks stupid enough to wander into the shallows to ravage my herd of crabs.

My best weapon was of course surprise, and stealth, but my crossbow might prove to be a close second. I had used the discharge lever from the fire extinguisher to make the bowstring release mechanism, and the bowstring was the cord that had been attached to the lever that released air from the top of the balloon and effectively saved me from floating off to a certain death at sea. The bow itself was a strip of steel from a mounting bracket for the balloon burners, and the stock was a disassembled section of aluminum tubing from the basket. All this was held together with more of that extremely useful nylon string from the basket, made fast with medical tape from the first aid kit.

The short arrows, or darts, were bamboo fletched with feathers. The occasional squad of boobies gathered at the south side of the island. Alas, one such bird succumbed to one of my arrows and sacrificed its plumage so that I could survive. No, I didn't even try to eat the booby, as I was dimly aware that sea birds are on par with scavenged octopus.

Sitting in my duck blind, I found that I could fire darts through the observation slot should an unfriendly approach. Yet I did not have a lot of confidence in my skill to actually put an arrow into an object. So I had a target I could set up on the beach made from two sticks with black nylon stretched between, and tied with nylon string. With time, my aim improved. My arrows traveled modestly well to the point where I could reliably hit the target within a foot or so of my aim at what I paced off as sixty feet. Beyond that, my arrows would not fly true enough for me to strike the target with any reliability.

The sixty-foot spot was marked with two square rocks.

I dare say that had I not had nylon string, my entire tale would be beyond grim. I used it to secure almost everything, from the jugs I used to collect rainwater off the tarps to an improvised tooth brush. The balloon basket had a seemingly endless supply woven through the wicker.

A shout-out is also due to the blessed whomever tossing their garbage into the sea and sending me all manner of plastic bottles and jugs to the eastern shore of the island. Too bad metal cans and pots don't float, as I could have used some of those.

Most notably, that string formed the basis of fishing line, both whole and stripped down to long nearly-transparent fibers. I had completed my rudimentary fly rod and had found some most entertaining angling in the flats. Hooks were fashioned using the balloon's decent lever. I would capture the edge of heavy steel staples and press them into shape against a rock. I used string fibers to lash booby fluff to the shank. For cement, I used melted nylon fibers. Along with coconut husk fiber antennae, I created fishing flies that looked much like a small mysid or shrimp.

One might imagine that I simply tied the line to the end of the rod and just threw enough line to hook stray palm-sized reef fish. The problem I encountered with this approach was that even a modestly–sized ocean fish is often much stronger than, say, a freshwater bluegill. My flies had no barbs, and so without the capacity to let line out and retrieve it, most of the fish I snagged tore the hook from their mouths or wriggled free.

Using more staples I fashioned metal guides on the sixteen foot cane pole through which I could release and retrieve line. No, I was not able to make a fishing reel, but most anglers would be amazed at how versatile simply wrapping the line around one hand can be. A tad awkward, to be sure, and extremely fast fish like bonefish would have broken me off (and certainly would have lined me), but it was adequate tackle for the small jacks and runners I plucked from the reef, which were tasty fare and easy to roast on sticks over coconut coals.

The occasional large trevally and milk fish would make appearances, and I pined for actual fishing tackle that might have made this episode an epic – albeit rustic in the extreme – fishing jaunt. Yet I had to let them pass, as my tackle would never be up to the challenge and I didn't fancy losing flies, which were deucedly hard to fashion without a proper fly tying vise.

The bounty of the sea was keeping me in decent shape food-wise.

Yet bat meat beckoned.

My crossbow was just the ticket.

Without elaborating with detail that could make some squeamish, I will just say that there isn't a lot of meat on giant fruit bats. They have an overabundance of wing. The flesh was sinewy. I steaked what I could, ending up with what looked like strips of lean, tough beef. Under normal circumstances, I would have marinated this type of game, hedging my bets (or bats, as the case may be) that this could only improve the taste.

Ingenuity bore many fruits on Toad Caye, not the least of which was in the beverage department. My boogle wine experiment yielded decent results that was enhanced by my discovery of peppercorn vines and wild clove. So I was able to marinate the bat strips in bitter boogle wine, pepper and clove. I had also mastered making salt by putting sea water onto a black tarp and letting it dry on the lea southwestern beach (even a slight breeze would blow sand into my salt.)

The anticipation for my bat feast grew as the smell of the grilling meat wafted gloriously from the glistening skewers. This called for not just wine but a cocktail.

Indeed, I had made a rudimentary solar still. I surrounded a large detergent bottle with the black basaltic native rock, which by midday became quite warm – warm enough to cause the ethyl alcohol to vaporize slowly and rise into an aluminum elbow from the basket frame. This elbow was shaded, which made it cool enough that the rising alcohol vapor would condensate and drip out of the end of the tube into another jug. The result was a small, precious supply of boogle brandy.

From my coconut shell cocktail cup I sipped the strong drink, admiring the aroma of grilled meat. It smelled no less delicious than the smell of grilled mystery meat from the carts on the streets of New York, though I guessed that the taste of bat could only be better.

While I waited for the dinner bell, I took the opportunity of direct late-day sunlight on my face to inspect my countenance in the silver blade of my no-longer-ceremonial sword. I kept my hair in a ponytail most of the time under the pith helmet. My beard and mustache was kept trimmed with the help of a sharpened strip of metal from the burner assembly. Trimmed whiskers was a concession to vanity and maintaining some sort of civilized appearance.

Tanned to the hilt, I noted that I was developing lines in my face that were not there before, especially around the eyes from squinting. No Ray Bans on Toad Caye.

My white military tunic and pants were frayed and of course no longer white and more like a tan olive. All I could do was wash them in sea water and none of the detergent bottles that washed ashore had any product within them. My undershorts were long gone, and to keep from chafing in trousers stiff with sea water I had to keep my inner thighs well lubricated with coconut oil. I know, too much information, but these are problems that I never imagined I would have. Over time, the inner thighs of my breeches became impregnated with oil, which helped. To look at me, you would have thought my pants were equipped with chaps.

I no longer wore shoes as I had developed sufficient callouses to get around without them and even scamper around on the volcanic rocks by the tide pools.

Fleas were an issue. I dug a sizeable depression under the hot sulfur spring and lined it with black nylon to create a tub. Twice a week I would soak in it to scare the blighters off. Likewise, that had a tendency to restore my body odor to a tolerable level. I had no idea how to make soap and so would scrub myself down with fresh, soft green leaves for the chlorophyll.

At last, the moment of gastronomical truth. I shed tears of delight when I chewed and chewed the tough, stringy, tangy spiced bat kabobs. Hard to imagine, I know, but had haggis or head cheese or Vienna sausage cans fallen from the sky I would likely have been equally enthralled. Likely I possessed some sort of nutritional need for animal fats that drove me to this bat satay bacchanal, but the experience was unparalleled.

And no, bat does not taste like anything else, and is a red meat. That the critters only eat fruit should give you a hint of the flavor.

Feast complete, I lolled in my deck chair – the one I'd made from basket wicker and balloon nylon – and surveyed the western horizon as I did every evening, the sun low over the glistening blue water and frothy waves breaking over the reef.

As I gazed at the sinking sun each evening, I no longer thought of anything about all that nonsense with Zarenga Chi, or the women – all irrelevant.

My libido seemed to have switched off while I was in emergency survival mode, too, which was a relief.

Thoughts were reserved for fishing the reef, when the next tide would go out and when it might rain next.

I killed and ate what I killed.

I collected water and I drank it.

An airliner twinkled against the darkening sky, a contrail in its wake, and I gave it no more notice than the terns pinwheeling over the frothing reef.

I had come to live, as they say, in the moment, in the hour, and by the rise and fall of the sun and tides. If I never left Toad Caye, I was OK with that, mostly, yet I didn't give it much thought as I had no control in that regard. There was nothing I could do but continue to live.

Funny, but I had attained a certain quietude of a sort I always wanted, but doubtless never would have found in civilized surroundings.

Not for long, anyway.

CHAPTER 20

GUNSHOTS NIPPED THE BREEZE.

I heard that unmistakable distant crack echo off the rocks.

Few moments in my life have been so instantly galvanizing.

Pirates.

I knew things were about to change, and in astounding ways.

The sun was high and bright as I raced for the forest edge, sand flying in my wake, my rod and string of fish flopping at my sides.

Maneuvering around the tree shadow, I cocked an eye through the branches and saw a small white ship flying the tricolor flag of France. It was anchored just beyond the reef opening. Surrounding it were smaller blue and grey boats – the ones the pirates used with large outboards.

Coming toward the Toad Caye through the reef opening was a bright orange Zodiac inflatable with two people in it.

Far behind them, a pirate boat was giving chase, and gaining.

Ditching my rod in the brush, I scampered along my emergency side trail up the rock stair to my camp and tossed the fish aside. I cupped my eyes and stared down at the approaching boats.

Two white people without guns were in the orange Zodiac.

Thin black men with guns were in the boat behind it.

It was clear to me that the small white ship had been surrounded and likely taken by pirates, while the two people in the Zodiac had decided upon escape.

Snatching up my cross bow and quiver of darts, I leapt from safe spot to safe spot down the front path to my duck blind, eyeing my trip wires along the way and relieved to see that most of them were still set.

I skidded to a kneeling position behind my blind, the orange Zodiac scrunching up onto the beach five hundred feet distant.

A man and a woman stood in the Zodiac – she in front was out first, and dashed to the forest line to the right of me.

There was a burst of gunshot, and some of the slugs buzzed overhead and smacked into the tree trunks.

The man in the Zodiac stumbled and fell out of the front of the boat.

He did not get up.

The woman stopped and looked back, swiping aside

a mane of dark, ringlet hair.

She screamed: "Antoine!"

And then she took a tentative step to run back to him.

I stepped out of the shadows into the sunlight where she could see me, jammed a pinky and forefinger in my mouth, and let loose a screeching whistle.

That hair swung violently as she focused on me: frozen, confused, and panicked.

I waved my arm for her to run toward me instead of the deceased Antoine.

The pirate boat slid up onto the beach next to the Zodiac, and the two lean black men squinted at me with obvious interest.

"Come on!" I shouted, my voice cracking.

Pivoting, she dashed toward me as the pirates hopped out of their boat. They did not run as she did, merely strode, likely because they assumed we were trapped on the island and they could easily find and capture us.

Or kill us.

A pirate shouldered his weapon and fired a shot at her and the slug smacked into the tree next to me.

I crouched back down in the duck blind and rock pile.

A second later she ducked into the forest and lunged, pulling her down next to me in the blind.

The two pirates were laughing, and joked in a language I did not understand as they approached. In baggy shorts and basketball jerseys, they did not seem like pirates. The one on the left had dreadlocks, and the one on the right had a shaved head and a flat, broken nose.

One of them sprayed the forest and duck blind with a burst of gunfire, slugs pinging off the rock pile in front of us.

Waiting, I began to feel their footfalls in the ground.

Wait. Wait for them to hit that sixty-foot marker, those two square stones. You won't have another chance.

The girl was hard to my side and trembling violently, stifling sobs. The fragrance of her shampoo, which was floral, reminded me of ylang-ylang flower. None such on Toad Caye.

I checked my crossbow to make sure everything was set and ready. It was loaded with one of the arrows tipped with a nail I harvested from a piece of drift wood.

Gritting my teeth, I rose up to the slot in the blind and aimed at the pirate on the left, the one with dreadlocks, the one who was laughing with an open mouth.

He was closer than my sixty foot marker. Fifty feet away?

I pulled the trigger.

The arrow went high and away from the center of his body.

Yet it didn't miss.

The shaft of the dart protruded from his open mouth, blood coursing down the shaft and onto the white sand. Eyes wide with utter disbelief and confusion, he turned toward his fellow pirate, the one with the shaved head and dented nose. He looked back at Dreadlocks in shock, mouth agape.

I could see the nail protruding from the back of Dreadlock's neck.

Loading another arrow, I took aim at Shaved Head.

Damn. Too low. Overcompensated.

Yet I didn't miss.

The arrow found its mark above the knee.

Dreadlocks had dropped his rifle and yanked the arrow out of his mouth, a gush of blood in its wake as he sank to his knees.

Shaved howled with pain, and swung his rifle.

I ducked.

There was a sort burst of fire that pinged the rocks and ripped the trees.

I could hear Dreadlocks gagging and gurgling.

Shaved cursed.

I popped up again to see Shaved struggling with his gun, pulling the magazine, seeing that it was empty.

My third arrow missed him entirely, but he knew enough at that point that he'd better run, so he did, as best he could with the arrow sticking out of his knee. He made tracks for his boat.

I said to the girl, her face buried in the leaf litter: "Stay."

I stood, sword in hand, and marched towards where Dreadlocks lay writhing in agony on the beach, a mixture of sand and blood matting his face and hair.

When he saw me coming he fumbled for his rifle. I took a few quick strides forward and rammed the blade of my sword into his chest, which clearly knocked the wind out of him.

I did it again.

Then once more for good measure. I wanted to make sure I lanced his heart and lungs.

This was Boone Linsenbigler killing a man dispassionately.

This was not the Boone Linsenbigler I had grown up as and not the Boone Linsenbigler I had been a year before.

To kill – either to eat or to keep from being killed – was now life.

The man gurgling his last before me was no more than a fish or a bat or a conch snail.

I was just surviving, and Dreadlocks was trying to interfere with that, so he, too, must die so that I could live.

His gun was caked in blood and sand from his chest wound, and I had no confidence that it would fire in that condition. So I snatched up my nail-tipped arrow from beside him and wiped the blood off it on his pant leg and loaded it into my crossbow. I strode jogged toward Shaved, who gagged with pain as he shoved his boat back into the water and clambered aboard.

His eyes brimmed with terror, and his mahogany skin and head glistened with sweat. The boat starter whirred, and the motor coughed to life.

I was fifty feet from him.

I took aim.

The arrow went wide.

It missed and sliced into the water next to the boat as it lunged away.

Shaved pointed a vengeful finger and shouted: "Freddie come back for you one day! You see!"

I watched impassively as he motored away, and then waded past the small breakers to retrieve my arrow.

Turning my attention to Antoine, I found that indeed he was dead, shot through the back of the head. This did not make for a pretty picture, so I rolled him face down and straight out on the beach so I could pull off his pants, shirt and belt. He was wearing sandals in my size, which was good fortune. While my feet were well calloused, sandals would help walking around the edge of the sharp coral.

A sudden pain in my ear was the result of the woman hitting me with her fists, screaming in French.

I pushed her away, and she gestured at Antoine stomping her foot and gesticulating wildly, clearly upset that I was harvesting whatever he no longer needed for what I might need.

It's no secret I'm not much good at languages. Oh, I've gotten by knowing some Russian phrases, curse words and insults. I know a couple of words in Spanish, too, enough that, with lots of hand gestures, I can communicate with Mexican fishing guides.

However, I took French in high school, a language

that I consider as an adult completely useless. French-speaking fishing guides were few and far between. Yet I had studied four-and-a-half years of French. I was bad at it twenty-five years before, and I was certainly no better now and having not spoken much of any language for months and months. The one time I tried to use French in far-northern Canada I asked a grocer where his pants were, and if they were fresh.

This skinny woman with the penetrating black eyes and black ringlet hair was spitting on me, yet I managed to put together the following, unedited for grammatical correctness, bellowing:

"Tout chose important ici, n'est pas? On besoin tout chose!" ("All things important here, isn't it? One needs all things!")

I waved a hand at the island and at myself. Then I pointed at Antoine: *"Il est morte, ça va? Nous sont ...um...n'est pas mort. D'accord?"* ("He's dead, right? We are not dead, OK?")

These pronouncements caused her to step back and merely weep uncontrollably. She tried to say something further but could not. With a yelp of anguish, she sank to her knees and crawled over to Antoine's body, her face down on his still shirted back, sobbing.

If I seem unmoved by this, I was. Sobbing and her anguish was pointless.

I left her and drifted back to examine the contents of the Zodiac, one eye watching Shaved/Freddie motoring for the ship. If they came back in force, I would need more than whatever ammo was left in Dreadlock's rifle to fend them off.

My advantage of surprise had been spent.

The Zodiac had a twenty-horsepower Mercury outboard and an external nine gallon plastic gas tank. My immediate thought was that I could fish outside the reef with this craft but I'd have to make a sturdier rod and stouter line for the larger fish.

Everything looked useful, from the fuel hose to the emergency supply container. The boat was clearly meant not only as a way to ferry people to shore but as a potential life raft. The emergency supply container had rations in the form of food bars, which I detest because I ate so many of them in Kazakhstan. There was bottled water, a whistle, a first aid kit and a flare gun. There was a hand fishing line and barbed hooks, which made me grin – at last, barbs for my flies! There was a GPS distress beacon, yet when I tried to activate the blasted thing the 'on' light did not illuminate. I opened the battery compartment and found that the power source was dead and had leaked acid. *Worthless.*

The gas tank was almost full. Yet it only contained nine gallons, and I had no idea how far that would take me across open ocean.

No doubt parts of the motor would make good arrow points, maybe have parts to improve my distilling operation. On second thought, perhaps I would want to keep it intact for an escape, or to motor toward a friendly craft passing nearby.

Squinting in the direction of the ship, I saw that Freddie had reached it and was tied up next to her.

On deck, I saw the distinctive wink of distant binoculars trained on me.

Take a good look, Laddie Buck. Boone will defend Toad Caye to his dying breath...or better still, yours.

CHAPTER 21

"MON DIEU!" WERE HER FIRST NON-ABUSIVE WORDS.

She said them upon entering my swish camp on the ledge. Perhaps the utterance of dismay was not directed at the swankiness of all the black nylon, fire ring, and impressive collection of plastic bottles arranged by size next to my sulfurous tub. Perhaps her 'My God!' was an expression of her dismay at seeing the amassed junk.

Her first question: "How long have you been here?"

I shrugged, and leaned Dreadlock's rinsed-off rifle against the rock face: *"Je ne connais pas."* ("I don't know.")

What I got from her next was, I think, "Your pronunciation is poor but I understand you."

Just because she had to suffer through my French doesn't mean we all have to. Going forward I'm going to relate mostly what I think I said and what I think she said, paraphrasing.

Old habits perish when you perish. I asked the lady entering my abode: "Would you like a drink?"

I saw the dark eyes scan my array of bottles

doubtfully. My guess was that she was around thirty five, and thin, but not a bean pole like some of the models you see lurching around the streets of Manhattan. When she ran up the beach I noted nicely rounded calves, and a level of athleticism, which would do her well if we remained marooned together for long. A head shorter than me, her face was graced with delicate features and narrow jaw, though her little nose was crooked. The small curvy lips were expressive ones that telegraphed how she felt. At that moment, I believe, they were twisted to the side, apprehensive about the quality of liquor I might have on hand.

Before she could answer, I poured her a slug of brandy into a cup made from the bottom of a water bottle. It was my finest cocktail glass.

She took the cup from me and smelled, then her eyes met mine. "Whisky? You make whiskey here?"

"I'm Boone Linsenbigler."

Eyes wide she took a step back and sank into my ramshackle lounge chair. Without taking her eyes off me, she downed the brandy in one gulp, and wheezed. "But you are dead!"

My reply was simply a smirk.

Then my eyes drifted beyond her to the ship and little boats, and I nodded toward them. "They're leaving."

She spun around in her chair, hand over her mouth. When she turned back, her eyes searched mine. "Do you have no way off this island? We are stuck here?"

Nodding, I said: "I guess they left because it wasn't

worth the trouble to kill us, or risk getting killed to kill us." I poured myself some brandy in my coconut shell and crouched in front of her. I had gotten very good at crouching comfortably – one does without chairs. "But it's better here than on that ship. How did you come this way? Nobody comes this way but pirates, and me."

Her eyes welled up with tears. "It's an ecological expedition. We have been doing biodiversity inventories on all the French protectorate islands like this one. We do this every three years to see what plants and faunae exist and estimate the population. In this way we study the impact of rising seas and warming climate, as well as pollution and over-fishing."

I snorted. "There are a lot less conch than the last time you were here. Why did you come without some sort of armed escort?"

"Our escort ship was called away to deal with pirates attacking another vessel." She put her face in her hands and sobbed – just once – before going silent, her mane of black ringlets closing in around her hands.

"How far is the nearest inhabited island, do you know? And which direction?"

"We left port two days ago. I do not think that the orange boat will take us that far."

My appetite for navigating the open seas was already spotty. In a little open craft with nine gallons of gas, the prospect of venturing out there was nauseating.

Finally she looked up at me, her lower lip protruding. "So what are we to do?"

I glanced out at the ocean. "You can see I've been here awhile. Nobody knows I'm here, but someone now might think that you are. If your expedition ship is rescued, perhaps your comrades will send a rescue. Then again, the pirates may hold onto your vessel for a long time waiting for a ransom. Then again, the pirates may come back here, just for fun, and try to kill us."

Her jaw tightened. "At least *you* they would just kill."

"No reason you can't go down fighting. What's your name?"

"Sophie. Sophie Dura. I am a botanist. But I am not strong enough to fight men like these."

I stood. "Not yet you can't, but you will, I've been expecting pirates and have this island rigged with traps and hidden paths. Look, Sophie, now that you're here in the same situation as I, you need to think differently. If you spend your time and emotional energy thinking about rescue, if you spend time thinking about home and family, you will starve and go mad."

She hung her head. "I will try."

"You have to focus on survival. That means food, water, shelter and self-defense. I have mastered the last three, but I will need your help to gather food for two people rather than one. And then there are the little things like washing, knowing where the latrine is, keeping the fleas away..."

"You have fleas?"

"Not at the moment. I take baths in there, with sulfur. You can drink that water also but the rainwater is much better. Which is another thing, we need more bottles to collect more rain water for the two of us. You can't rely on it to rain frequently, but when it does, we need to store as much water as possible."

"So, Linsenbigler, you floated all the way here from Zarenga Chi in the balloon? They said you were lost at sea. This was news even back in France."

I nodded. "And much of what you see around you came from that balloon – yards and yards of black nylon."

"Things do not go well in Zarenga Chi since you died. The corporations are trying to replace the monarchy with an autocracy and the citizens form large protests. There are riots."

"I don't suppose there was any news about Vladimir Putin owning their banks and treasury? About Putin money laundering through their banks?"

She just seemed puzzled, wiggling her pursed lips. Then she shook her head, her gaze drawn to the ocean, the aqua blue reflected in her eyes. "I can't believe this is happening." The tears started again. "And my co-workers, my friends, the people in my expedition, I can't bear to think what they are going through, or whether any more are dead. Poor Antoine. He was so brave to take the boat and come to the island. Maybe it was foolish. Certainly for him it went badly."

"Was Antoine your lover?"

"No, I have a…I'm…" Without looking at me she shook her head. "No."

"Sophie, I'll give you some time to grieve, but I will need you to help me, to help us survive here."

She nodded, looking at her hands, and I continued.

"You stay here. I have to get rid of the pirate's body, and Antoine's. Do you have any objections to burying him at sea, wrapping him in nylon and sinking him out beyond the reef? To dig a grave would use too many calories. And it's pretty rocky here."

Groaning, she shook her head and waved her hand, her curvy little lips tight. "I will dig the grave. He was my friend."

"All I have for a shovel is that plank over there. I suggest you find a spot around to the south, about ten minutes walking. The soil is softer there. I'll wrap the body, bring it over by boat and then drag him up the beach. There's no way I can carry him."

She stood and retrieved the driftwood plank, wiping tears from her face with a forearm. "Do you have something I can use to tie my hair back?"

I plucked one of the many lengths of string hanging on a nearby tree and handed it to her. She was dressed in navy tank top, tan shorts, and sandals – that would not be sufficient garb for an extended stay at Toad Caye. When she reached back with both arms to bunch her hair and tie it, my libido made a guest appearance when I saw the shape of her small breasts press into the front of her tank top. She also had a lovely, gently curving nape – I don't know how many men admire that part of a woman's anatomy, but my hat's in the ring.

Hair tied back and chin resolutely high, she blinked tears from her eyes and said: "Show me the way down to the beach. I must learn this so not to trigger any of the traps you showed me on the way up."

We hopped and zigged down the path, and then she marched away down the beach with the plank, lithe arms swinging. I spent a moment marveling at how alien women are from men in shape and function. Had I forgotten in a matter of months?

I guessed I had.

With rope looped under Dreadlock's armpits, I dragged him down to the Zodiac. He stank, and his clothing was filthy and not worth harvesting. I checked his pockets and they contained only an amulet inscribed with Sanskrit. No doubt it was inscribed with the name of The Prophet, a good luck charm.

Not so much.

Ah, the miracle of technology! An outboard motor that wasn't made of black nylon or string or coconut shells or plastic bottles. I had not ventured beyond the reef while on Toad Caye, out to where the water turned a darker blue. Towing the carcass through the breach, I cut Dreadlock loose where the fish and turtles could have their way with him, his amulet in his pocket – perhaps it would take him to a better place.

The shimmer of the deeper, sultry water was mesmerizing. I watched the body sink slowly into the broken shafts and curtains of sunlight.

Pooled blood rose in a long wisp from the dead

man's chest like smoke from a cigarette.

A dark, familiar silhouette with chevron fins curved around the body. As much as I fear being confronted by sharks, I do not fear them when safely separated from their environment.

Then another joined the first, and they and the body slipped out of sight like shadows into night.

CHAPTER 22

I RECOMMEND BEING MAROONED WITH A BOTANIST.
Sophie's training helped supplement the larder with
variety. We now had some root vegetables in the mix, as
well as wild ginger, which also put a zing in the wine to
help balance the sour of the boogles. She had the proper
name for my boogles, but I wouldn't have it, they were
mine, and I named them. My obstinacy on this
technicality became a game of sorts whereby she insisted
on calling them by the correct name and I by my name.
We each would try to get the other to acknowledge the
fruit by the other person's identifier.

Hand me a boogle, please?

A what?

One of those.

This, Mr. Linsenbigler?

That, Ms. Dura.

So you want a whatsit, is that what you're saying?

No, I'd prefer a boogle.

Not exactly laugh-out-loud funny, but under the

sobering circumstance of being stranded, any joke in a storm.

Sophie had taken to wearing Antoine's long sleeve shirt against the sun, and had woven a palm frond hat that she shaped by soaking it in sea water and then drying tied over a rock that matched the size of her head. Not exactly a milliner's finest creation, but on her it looked quite stylish. She mostly kept her black ringlet mane tied back in a ponytail, that as the weeks passed grew longer, as did mine.

I set about teaching her where I collected the conch, and where I fished, and where the boogles were and the coconuts, which were becoming scarce. Sophie had dark moments, especially as night fell, when she stared at the coals in silence, a tear tumbling down her cheek. Fortuitously, she mostly dwelt on the task at hand of survival, and earnestly listened and learned what I had discovered over the months. When it rained – day or dark of night – she helped fill water bottles as fast as we could from the tarp. When I brought fish, she cleaned them before I had the chance. She combed the beach for drift wood, bottles and whatever else looked useful. We worked together to fashion her a bed and mattress from nylon stuffed with dried palm fronds. I made her a toothbrush.

A couple weeks in, I sensed she was in estrus, as she was experiencing cramps that at first I naively thought were caused by the food. That was tough for her in those environs without modern conveniences, and I told her to take it easy until she was over it.

Then I saw her scratching, and she looked balefully at me, those little lips twisted to one side: "I need to take a bath." Fleas.

I grinned, and waved a hand at the ocean and beach. "Welcome to paradise!"

We didn't enact much ceremony about her slipping into the warm, sulfurous pool. I kept my back turned, for the most part, but she did not seem overly modest, Sophie's comparatively small body fitting much better than mine in the tub. I handed her the soft green leaves I use to bathe, and she asked for my crude razor, using it and coconut oil to scrape her armpits and trim her bush, places the fleas like to camp.

When she emerged, there was no towel to dry off so her pale comely French bottom disappeared around the end of the camp. She climbed around the side of the tarp and up onto the rocks to dry in the sun.

All very sexy, isn't it? No doubt some would imagine this predicament an obvious fulcrum for amorousness. Not obvious at all without the creature comforts of toiletries and toothpaste and fluffy white Turkish towels. In its natural state, in the tropics, the human body is at turns salty, sweaty and smelly. Hair is oily and tangled. Nails are jagged and dirty. This state of affairs discourages close, personal contact.

Not the least of the privations, with regards to intimacy, was a lack of birth control. A pregnancy would be a disaster in that environment.

Yet now that I had company, I took time to swim in the ocean after fishing to help keep my odor in check.

I set about familiarizing her with the crossbow and imparting instruction on fashioning the arrows, carefully plucking just the right straight feathers from the booby pelt hanging on the tarp post.

Once she had some practice with the weapon, I led her to the grove of trees where the bats roosted during the day.

She gasped, pointing up into the cool canopy. *"Ah, les chauve souris!"*

I replied: *"Repas ce soir."* ("Tonight's dinner.") I had thought it best to ease her into this particular part of Toad Caye's menu.

"You are not serious!"

"Mais oui. Ne pas knock it until you try it. Allons-y. Shoot one."

She paused, her probing dark eyes searching mine from under that frond hat, her faced framed in black ringlets.

"Vous les mange?" ("You eat them?")

"Oui. Muy bien." Sometimes Spanish crept in to my translations, which was fine because she spoke some Spanish as well as French – just not much English.

She tilted her hat back and took aim at the closest one, the pink of her tongue peeking out between her curvy little lips. The forth arrow hit its mark, and the critter squawked, falling to the forest floor. Bats nearby peeked down at us from behind their wings and hissed.

I directed Sophie to find the arrows that missed, though making sure she took care to avoid the vines and conch shells I had strewn about the forest floor. The bat grove was one of my potential escape routes and I wanted any pursuers to encounter as many tripping hazards as possible. Sophie had not moved twenty feet before she stumbled: *"Zut!"* ("Darn it!")

I found the felled bat and dispatched it fully with my sword. Decapitation was the safest and least gruesome method. They quickly bleed out, and I didn't risk being bitten if they weren't fully dead. Puncturing the body would run the risk of rupturing internal organs that might taint the meat.

When she returned (having only found one of the missing three darts) she was quite excited. *"Tamarin!"* She was pointing from whence she came, so I scooped the dead bat into a black nylon sack and followed her. (The bats had fleas so it was not wise to handle them directly until the insects had been smoked out of the pelt over hot coals.)

Sure enough, Sophie had found a tamarind tree, the long seed pods dangling from the branches. When I first walked through that part of the island along the Toad's back, the tree had not been in seed so I did not know what it was. For the uninitiated, tamarind pods look like longer versions of the seed pods on a locust tree, which are very common in America, and especially in New York. Tamarind seed are coated in a sticky red-brown fiber that is both sweet and tart and nutritious. It is also an obscure cocktail ingredient with which I had experimented with little success. I had tried scraping the juicy parts into cheesecloth and then soaking it in a neutral spirit to come up with an infusion. It tasted like dirt, so I had resolved to try cooking the mush the next time. But there was no next time. Sloth prevailed – you can buy tamarind syrup that's quite tasty without all the effort of making it yourself.

"Aidez moi, Boone." She held out her arms, and I crouched down and cradled her foot, hiking her up into the tree.

Odd as it may seem, witnessing her naked taking a bath had not roused my sleeping libido. It was roused, however, when I felt her velvety skin on mine. Her exposed stomach was against my face, and then her legs. I had to reach up and put a hand on her plush little bottom to help her into the crotch of the tree. For the first time in months, since Foresh, I felt a certain feral longing, and I don't mind saying that I wished I hadn't.

That from Boone Linsenbigler, a veritable pillar of virtue?

While it has been amply demonstrated that I am an ardent fan of intimacy, there is a time and a place. You know when it's opportune and you know (generally) when it isn't. Under normal operating procedures, the S.S. Linsenbigler would steam right into port. Yet stranded on an island with an attack of hostile forces imminent, I couldn't afford to be distracted, or to let my guard down, or to have my judgement clouded. Were I an actual 'man of action,' I would not question my faculties. Indeed, I was succeeding at survival, and I beat the pirates back once…but next time? And the stakes were higher. This wasn't just me, it was Sophie. Whether I liked it or not, as the more experienced and stronger hunter-gatherer on Toad Caye, I felt responsible for her safety.

Sophie scrambled the rest of the way up and stood looking down at me, panting from the exertion, a flickering smile under her little crooked nose, one eyebrow slightly cocked. If I didn't know better – and I didn't – I think we both experienced a moment of longing. Or she was just mocking mine – I may have blushed.

The moment passed as she made like a monkey, scrambling along the large tree limbs and knocking down seed pods, me below snatching them up.

Back at camp, she shucked the pods and wiped the paste from the seeds into a growing pile of reddish-brown pulp. This took some time, and when she was done she mashed the paste around sticks and lay them on rocks in the sun.

I prepared the bat, smoking the fleas from the pelt and then making the marinated skewers as before. Without refrigeration, I didn't have the luxury of marinating them for very long, and I used the new wild ginger root Sophie had found.

We sat in our makeshift lawn chairs to eat facing the sea from our promontory, each with a plastic tumbler of boogle wine.

Sophie held one of my bat skewers at arm's length, admiring it. "It smells and looks wonderful, but I wonder if I would have said so a month ago." Biting off a chunk, she chewed, the little lips rotating as she did so. "It doesn't taste anything like chicken. It's like the skewered meat at Asian restaurants. Tough, but good. Not sure of the wine pairing."

She was right, it tasted like those skewers one finds in a pu-pu platter.

The tamarind skewers were a treat by far. Anything sweet on the island, other than coconut, was sour. This was downright candy, and I felt the boost of energy.

When done we threw our skewers in the fire and sat back with a brandy to watch the sun set.

We had talked very little of anything personal in all those weeks, mainly because there was so much to discuss on a practical level for the ins and outs of survival. That, and we had communication difficulties, but those had eased over time. Perhaps that evening the wine and brandy got the better of us.

"Boone, how do you go from being that person on television to this?"

I was caught so off guard that I honestly did not know what she meant, and said so. She elaborated:

"Even in France I had seen something of you in advertisements, and items in the news. I thought all this was acting and made up by publicity people, with the sword fights and all that, but here you are making cross bows and killing pirates and eating bats. They said you would be king of Zarenga Chi."

I heaved a great sigh, my eye on the horizon. "It's not by choice, I can tell you that. I didn't ask to be king, and I certainly never wanted to be here."

"Now that I know you, it is hard for me to imagine you any other way than this, with your pith helmet and sword and tattered uniform. I'm sorry if that offends you."

I took a healthy swig of my brandy, meeting her eyes briefly. "There was a time – not so very long ago – that I was what one calls 'a nobody.' I was a freelance writer scrounging out a living writing fishing articles and posting cocktail recipes on Facebook pages, hanging around in dive bars, waiting for my ship to come in."

She laughed softly, shaking her head. "I would have liked to have known you then."

"Looking back, I think I knew somehow something big was going to happen but I never imagined becoming a brand, much less all this unrelenting trouble."

"Trouble or misfortune?"

"Both. You see, once you become famous, everybody wants a piece of your fame to use for some other end. It was my bad luck to come to the attention of Vladimir Putin."

"Oh, the fish explosions!"

"And once you get hoodwinked into the whole world of intrigue, well, it's difficult to escape. In Zarenga Chi, I had two choices: become a compliant and complicit king or die. I didn't think they were that serious about the second part. I was warned, but I thought I had control of the situation." I waved my glass at our surroundings. "The result is this."

"Yet you escaped. You told me they tried to toss you in the volcano, but you escaped. And now all these months later, you have prevailed, you have control of the situation."

I cocked an eyebrow at her. "Have I? We'll see. Or maybe we won't. Maybe nobody will ever come here again. As you know, I try not to think about rescue. But I admit to becoming weary of this life here."

"But what will you do when you return?"

I grinned. "I've had a lot of time to think about that." I was tempted to go on, to tell her about the thumb drive, but I didn't dare. Anyone who knew about the thumb drive was likely to end up as I had, or worse. So I changed the subject. "And you? Do you have close family?"

Her brow knit, and her lips tightened. "My first day here you gave me some very sound advice. You told me not to think of such things as it is painful."

"I apologize, you're right, I shouldn't have asked. It sometimes just seems odd that here we are – friends, I'd say – and we know so little about each other. But let me ask this: assuming we ever get out of here, what will you take away from Toad Caye that you will use back in civilization?"

She laughed mirthlessly. "A renewed appreciation for soap, toilets, bidets, showers, towels…a renewed appreciation for everything about bathrooms, really. Boone, I need to thank you for all you've done for me. I don't think I ever have thanked you."

I snorted. "That's ridiculous, Sophie, you don't have to thank me. This is what it is. Events have a life of their own around me, and I just do the best I can with what confounded situation life conjures next. To be honest, I should thank you for being stranded here with me. I was going a little too feral all by myself. Not that I would have wished this on anybody."

"I know what you mean, and in a way, I'm happy that I'm here to help you."

I turned to face her. "You can't mean that, Sophie. This situation is all at my feet, not yours, and it's my burden."

"The pirates were both our situation, Boone. With all that has happened to you, there seems to be some kind of destiny at work. That doesn't mean that along the way you don't need help."

"Oh, please, don't say that." I was harking back to Beamish, the butler and spy, and his parting words in Istanbul's fog. "I don't believe any of that fate and destiny talk. I can't."

"And you talk of your 'burden?' What is that but your fate? Have you ever heard of the Fibonacci Sequence? This is the sequence of numbers that result from starting with zero and adding the next number to the one before it. The first number is zero plus one, which is one. The next is two, then two plus one or three. The next is five, then eight, then thirteen up to fifty-five and beyond. This sequence is a constant in botany. Flowers almost all have a number of petals corresponding to Fibonacci numbers. The number of swirls in the bottom of a pine cone, or the pattern of seeds in a sun flower, or the scale configurations in pineapples...they all fit the pattern. A pattern not of their own making, but of nature."

"How do these Fibonacci numbers have anything to do with me?"

"There are subtle patterns, forces in nature that are not understood. I saw in the paper, when you died at sea in the balloon, a picture of you in your uniform standing in front of a portrait of Maximillian von Lichtenbichler. There's a strong resemblance."

"Oh, so its reincarnation now, is it?"

"Not that. But perhaps the repeat of a pattern in nature. Genetics, but more than that." Her eyes were downcast into her brandy, a gentle smile on those little curvy, inquisitive lips. "There's something about you, Boone...I feel there's something special about you that goes beyond your body and mind. The ancient Greeks would have made you their Odysseus, it's like you have been chosen by the gods to endure a series of trials. But you can't see that or feel what I feel, so you just think you're a little jinxed at the moment."

I nearly spit out my drink. "A little jinxed? Just a little?"

She reached out a calming hand and placed it on my

cheek. It was slender and warm and strong. Yet not soft. There were callouses from our daily labors.

"I'm sorry. You will take this time here in isolation to map your fortunes going forward rather than allow yourself to be victimized by them. This I know."

The hand lingered, and I eased back into my chair with a groan. "How could you possibly know that?"

"I know it in my heart." She brought her hand back to her lap and heaved a short sigh, the huffing kind used to flush out strong emotion and switch gears. Her eyes quickly scanned the horizon and then landed on me.

"So when are you going to teach me to fly fish?"

CHAPTER 23

I AM A POOR FLY CASTING INSTRUCTOR. Previously, I've noted that the best way to teach fly casting is at the end of a cattle prod: *Do Not Bring the Rod So Far Back.* *TZZZZZT!*

Yet students say:

"Oh, I'm pretty athletic, I pick things up quickly, you wait and see."

Balderdash. What they usually pick up are a lot of bad casting habits and line wrapped around their heads because they think fly casting is roughly the same as riding a bicycle. It looks easy when I do it so they figure it must be easy to learn.

It is not. Why? Because unlike the intuitive balance and momentum it takes to master a bicycle, fly casting requires acute counterintuitive skills. To cast effectively, you have to attain a feel for how much the weight of the line in mid-flight behind you bends the rod. Based on how much the rod bends, you have to gauge how much forward motion of the rod in your hand is required to enact the spring action from the bent rod to propel the line forward smoothly. I don't think there's a word for feeling how much bend there is a in a rod – perhaps an alternate definition of *propinquity*? 'Rod feel' defies most attempts to explain it in words. Which is why watching your line in flight is an essential tool in attaining 'rod feel.' The bent rod is the principle mechanism that propels the line forward at the line's peak moment of resistance when curled out behind you. So if you witness that moment you can refine your timing. There's no primal mechanism in the inner ear or in your ability to throw a baseball, javelin, boomerang or stone that assists you. More force from your arm does not equal more distance.

Imagine if to throw a football downfield you had to release it behind you? It's that counterintuitive. As such, you have to attain the muscle memory and "feel" for the relationship between the bend of the rod and the weight of the line in the air.

Nobody just walks up and learns how to fly cast in a matter of hours.

Nobody except Sophie.

She watched intently from under her thatch sun hat, her black curls glistening in the reflection from the water and her lips pursed in rapt attention. She seemed to be actually listening as I explained how it works. You *lift the rod with force*, launching the line behind you, yet bringing the rod back only to just behind your ear in doing so. Then you pause to let the line loop out behind you and bend the rod. *Watch this happen.* Only then do you *press the rod forward,* bringing the rod tip forward to about a forty degree angle out in front of you. Note the words *lift* and *press*, which are not interchangeable with *jerk, yank, thrust, snatch, heave or wrench.*

Sophie's only comment inspired hope: "So it's mostly about how you throw the line backward, not forward."

Just so.

The dance of fly casting instruction is myriad, though I feel that you must put your arms around the student and hold their arms so that they learn what you mean by *lift* and *press,* which are made even less precise in my crude French translations. This learning huddle is of course easier if the person is smaller than you, or skinny and pretty like Sophie.

We stood on the lea side of the island so the wind would not interfere with the proceedings, and that when we stood in the pale blue shallows with white sand the waves wouldn't vex us.

Nestled in my arms, Sophie smelled of salt, sun and sea, the side of her sun hat folded against my face. I held her arms, the right holding the rod, the left hand with the line wrapped around it. She may have been skinny, but her arms were ropey, perhaps made so more by our daily exertions.

During the first cast, I felt her arms resist mine as they anticipated a motion or force other than what I was using to move her arms.

"*Encore,*" she said.

It was only after maybe the twentieth *encore* that she said flatly: *"D'accord."* OK.

I stepped back and watched her cast perfectly twenty times in a row, before she turned and asked: "Farther. I will not catch as many fish as you unless I can throw the line farther."

This is usually when the student falls flat on her face because she must now do three or four things at once instead of two. Typically, the resultant frustration leads to some bad casts, overcompensation, and line wrapped around the caster, and in some instances, tears. So I held my breath as I watched her step forward and try to throw line at the end of the cast as I instructed.

The crude fly and line sailed straight out to the edge of the deeper water, curling outward and neatly rolling the fly onto the surface of the water with a gentle *slap*. The fly sank slowly from view.

Nodding at the distant fly, she said: "This is not easy, but I understand it."

Her line jerked tight and she instinctively lifted the rod.

Fish on!

"Boone! La pêche!" She let loose a hoot of delight as the long cane rod throbbed.

Out of the water leapt a narrow silver fish about two feet long, the shape similar to a lady fish, though I did not know whether it was the same species we catch in the states.

Not only had she learned to cast decently in the first

lesson, and to throw line, but she had managed to hook a fish as well.

Astounding.

I tromped out into the water, instructing Sophie to keep the rod high, then to the side, and to wrap the line around her hand to bring the fish toward where I could grab it.

Once I had the gasping fish in hand, we both fell to our knees in the shallows laughing and astonished. Sophie inspected the fish closely, the subtle blue colors of the back and lateral line, the shape of the fins, the sparkle of its eye. *"Magnifique. Laisse le manger!"*

Magnificent! Let's eat it!

And so it was that I began to fashion Sophie her own fly rod, and together we did the wrappings and I showed her how to make the flies. Her slender fingers were much better than mine for making flies, and with four hands I could hold the hook (without the benefit of a fly tying vice) for her while she tied. The results were much better, much sturdier flies.

She even braided her own fly line, and knotted her leaders.

I have to say, looking back on it, even with all the privations of living off the land, those were halcyon days. In the bright tropical sun and crystal blue waters, the two of us made her tackle and stalked the edge of the reef catching fish. She laughed and squealed with delight at each hook up, chattering away in French that I could not understand – except that I know she was talking to the fish. Something like:

"Oh, you impetuous little gilled thing! You must be more careful! Sophie is here, and she is very dangerous, you must hide in the reef and not come out when you see her shadow. But it will be fine, I will eat you, and that is as it should be. You eat others, and I eat you, it is the way of the world, is it not?"

Hilarious. Well, I thought so.

And bless her, Sophie as scientist made some vast improvements to the still by creating a larger reservoir of wine that automatically fed the main still. Plus, we relocated the still into a thermal vent that we found in a rock crevice, speeding up the rate of the distillation process. We not only had more fish and more fun, but we had more boogle brandy. It was a little harsh (as you might imagine), but it was better than the boogle wine, which was bitter and prone to spoiling in the heat. A little clove and tamarind turned the brandy into a decent cocktail. I missed ice terribly.

So fish, the occasional bat barbeque, and cocktails with sunset, which was spent discussing the finer points of fly fishing. She wondered whether adding other elements to the flies like her hair or some of the blonde and silver of mine might make them better. She would tell me about the new plants she had identified during the day, which she memorized without paper using mnemonic system whereby she put the names of the plants to a song. So each evening she serenaded me with the most recent additions to her list, her lilting thin voice and Frenchie accent gracing Toad Caye.

A monsoon season began to set in, which was not a bad thing. It rained for maybe a day or two allowing us to fill an enormous number of bottles with drinking water. Truly a relief to have a large supply. Then the weather would clear for a few days.

I became less and less fearful that the pirates would return, or that anyone would stumble upon us anytime soon. Just the same, I kept the weapons close at hand and ready. I had re-thought my emergency plans, and had decided to fortify the ledge camp entrance by piling rocks along the edge where the path led down to the beach. Behind this stone pile, I stockpiled a dozen flimsy water bottles filled with the outboard motor's fuel. With the tops loosened or removed, they made decent Molotov cocktails if thrown and ignited. For that purpose, I brought the propane tanks and burners down from behind the camp on the rocks. I modified the burners so that the flames shot farther and had it mounted like a fire cannon in my little fortress. In this way I could ignite the burners and then toss the Molotov cocktails over the wall to try to erect a wall of fire below us, giving us ample time to go out the opposite way. We had established a back way from camp scrambling up over the top of the toad and down the far side to where we had the Zodiac camouflaged in the forest, complete with a supply of dried fish, water and those hideous food bars in case we needed to slip off the island and avoid the pirates all together.

If they came.

More pressing and real were concerns about our feet. Any small scratch would become infected quite easily during the monsoon, and Sophie theorized that bacteria or mold in the leaf litter on the path bloomed with the heavy rains. From her work in the tropics she was aware of jungle rot, which was an affliction of the extremities. It was fortunate that we had a topical antibiotic from the Zodiac's and balloon's first aid kits. Still, as a precaution, we wrapped our feet in black nylon coming and going from camp and soaked our feet in the warm sulfur water daily. A runaway infection for either of us would, of course, prove calamitous.

During that time, Sophie discovered a bottle on the beach that contained a small quantity of green liquid soap, and who would ever have surmised that this could create such excitement. We danced and hugged over the prospect of taking a shower. It rained that afternoon, and since all our water bottles were full, we stood together naked under the tarp drain and lathered ourselves silly. We really should have saved that soap for wound care, but saner heads did not prevail. The sun came out, and we dried naked on the rocks.

My eyes closed, I heard Sophie half-whisper: "I am curious what Boone smells like when he is clean. It may be my only chance."

I heard her draw near, and then I felt her nose on my neck, her breast on my arm, and when I opened my eyes, she was sniffing deeply up my ear and into my hair. *"Tu sens bon, Boone."* Her dark ringlets spilled slowly over my face.

I buried my face under the ringlets, nose in her nape, and she smelled heavenly: *"Toi aussi, Sophie."*

Heavenly?

She smelled like spring in New York, like cherry blossoms and tulips and azure skies and warm lawns.

She smelled of laughter and peace and contentment, and everlasting adoration.

She smelled of a gentle caress and longing looks.

That sniff of her nape?

And apparently one sniff of mine?

There was a brief moment in which our eyes met and we realized what was happening.

From above me, she gently pressed her lips to mine.

Our tongues touched.

Zeus threw no bolt of lightning hotter than that one. Passion sparked in us both, erupting in a firestorm.

Never have I had it happen so suddenly, or the bolt come from a clear blue sky.

It wasn't as if we had been flirting. There had been no innuendo, none of the usual *foreplay* foreplay. Not even propinquity! Well, I guess there had been, in the true meaning of the word.

The gush of emotion was organic, born from months of toil, companionship, teamwork, sharing and discovery.

This was not the garden from which a crocus springs forth impetuously through the snow. This was like an orchid that after time and care — after months and months of not blossoming no matter what you did – burst forth with the most stunning blossom you've ever seen.

So even though it seemed sudden, it was not, it had been building slowly and secretly. I, for one, did not see it coming.

I would not have thought in a thousand eons that this fantastic, smart, caring, skinny French woman with the little crooked nose, funny little mouth and cascades of dark ringlets would be one I would fall for.

But I did.

Unavoidable, when I think back on it.

As sudden as it was, it was also impossibly deep, the flames parting, and a chasm of love opening before us, we two falling.

Both of us could not stop whispering *"Je t'aime."*

I love you.

The catalyst?

An ounce of Palmolive dish soap.

They call it falling in love because there is no stopping once the gravity of desire pulls you into the chasm. So I could not stop and say: "This is a bad idea, Sophie, we're adults, after all, and we have to keep our priorities straight."

Last time in love? I was in my twenties.

I had forgotten what a glorious, terrifying storm love was. *Lash me to the wheel!*

A thunderhead rolled in, and amidst the clashes of thunder and flash of lightening, we ravaged each other on our two beds slid together. That kind of lovemaking is as if each is attempting to become part of the other, or form one being.

Impossible yet seemingly destined to be so.

Impossible not to be so.

Or maybe, just impossible.

Night fell.

We embraced by the red coals of the fire.

Sipping brandy.

Saying nothing.

And everything.

CHAPTER 24

"LINSENBIGLER! FREDDIE IS HERE!"

It was a man's accented shout, coming from a distance down the beach.

Freddie the pirate's shout.

It was predawn, first light, and I gently shook Sophie awake. She was curled in my arms, and sleepily reached up and touched my lips.

I whispered: *"Ne parle pas."* I gently put a hand over her mouth, and the voice from down the beach shouted again:

"Where is the man who would be King of Zarenga Chi? If you come out, we will not shoot you. But we will take you and sell you and get you off of this island."

We scrambled to a crouch, peering down at the beach, but they were too far away to the right to be seen yet.

I looked at Sophie and whispered in English: "How the devil do they know I'm here?"

My mind raced. Freddie got a good look at me when

he was last there. I suppose it took him this long to figure out who the hermit living on Toad Caye was, and to find his way back.

Our attention was suddenly drawn to the left, out beyond the reef.

Maybe a mile out a ship was steaming into view.

A light grey naval ship flying the French tricolor.

Freddie continued: "That frigate will not save you. They been chasing us, but when we have you, that is our ticket to freedom. So no play games. Is that girl still with you?"

"*Allons-y*" I whispered to Sophie, and we put on our sandals and headed out the back way toward the Zodiac. I slung the sword and scabbard across my back, and hefted Dreadlock's rifle.

Scrambling over rocks and down a steep rock face, we stumbled through the forest until we came to the edge of the mangrove, which was full with a flood tide. I set my rifle aside. The high tide was good because the Zodiac was afloat. We shoved the palm branch camouflage off the orange boat and into the water to the side.

Guiding the Zodiac to an opening in the mangroves, I gestured for Sophie to climb in. I kept walking the boat past the small breakers until the water was chest high. I hiked myself up so that I was sitting on the edge of the pontoon and I could prime and start the outboard.

It coughed to life, and I tried to limit the amount of noise it was making yet at the same time I didn't dare let it stall. Outboard motors can be deucedly hard to start again once they stall.

"*Ici.*" I waved Sophie over to the back of the boat. "You take this boat out to the frigate. The pirates want me, not you. They will not chase you if I remain here."

"*Non!*" She lunged, wrapping her arms around me. "You cannot. Boone, I am horrible, you cannot do this for me."

"It's the only way. If I go with you, they will have to chase us down, with faster boats, and they will take us hostage, and the navy will not be able to rescue us. This way, at least one of us gets away, but I think I can stall long enough that the navy will have time to come ashore."

She sobbed into my neck, and then pulled back, her face contorted with anguish. "Boone, I am married. And I have a child, a little girl, Camille. I did not tell you. I don't know why, but I did not, maybe because I didn't want to think of never seeing them again, maybe because to do so would make surviving impossible. Like you, I had to be all about here. Our island."

I believe there is science confirming that men and women think differently, and not just as a result of social influences. It has been demonstrated that the female brain is more free associative, that both lobes more freely communicate than those of their male counterparts. Men generally think in a narrower and more focused manner, which is why we are often confounded that females have the astounding capacity to pull thoughts from left field, and at junctures that utterly baffle us.

Or in this case, profoundly dishearten me.

She brings this up now? Not months ago? Not before I fell in love with her? Not before I had to go back and try to outwit pirates armed to the teeth, and me with just three rounds of ammo?

I shoved myself over the edge, back into the water, and gave the Zodiac a shove out toward the reef. "Go. I will see you later."

Sobbing, she took the tiller. *"Je t'aime, Boone!"*

Sophie put it in drive and vectored away toward the frigate, which had anchored. At high tide with an inflatable she would have no problem passing over the reef.

Back in the mangroves, I hefted the rifle, my heart in knots. I staggered, and I suppressed a sob.

Every man has a breaking point. I had become feral all alone on that island, and when Sophie came, I tried to remain that way, but companionship and then love...

Then love gone.

There was no kidding myself that she would leave her husband and child, or that I would entertain asking her to do so, or even condone it.

I was adult enough to know that for love to work, or work best, it needs to be unfettered. Well, let's just say that's the way I needed it to be. Yes, we'd fallen in love only the night before, but the taproot of that little tree ran far deeper than one encounter, we were far more attached to each other than we had known.

From those heights, the lows seem far lower.

I was suddenly losing it right when I needed most to

hold it together.

Sophie is lost to me, she is my better self. So, what is the point now of continuing to struggle? Were I to survive this, will there just be another drug kingpin or homicidal maniac or government after me? Maybe the best thing is to not use this rifle to save my life for more hell but to end my life and maybe find peace. After all, I'm jinxed, right? Kismet and the fates and all that malarkey have conspired against me to make me kill people and suffer all manner of slings and arrows of my outrageous fortune, but now this? Give me Sophie and take her away? Only to go back into the world and be double-crossed by the likes of women like Tanya and Foresh? What's the point?

A darker moment never shadowed my door.

I looked around me at the tangled plants, vines and leaf litter. It was as if I were looking at the disarray in my own heart. I wanted to burn it, torch the entire island, destroy my idiotic camp and tarps and string and tackle and weapons. In a single day, Toad Caye had become a giant monument to my pathetic, pointless existence, my pointless struggle.

What's the point?

The little silver canister with the thumb drive was cool against my sternum. Was it worth it to keep going for that, to take a chunk out of Putin and try to help Zarenga Chi? The whole damn world was a mess, and here I thought I could make one corner of it better? The man who lost Sophie, the ridiculous man dressed in rags who was stuck on this miserable island, is that the man who can make some sort of difference, other than bringing silly cocktail amenities into people's pantries? The imbecile who once thought a tropical hideaway was the answer to his problems rather than the culmination of them?

I sank to my knees, slowly sliding the rifle barrel under my chin. *Can I do this?*

How can I not?

This was the sort of time one of my father's idiotic sayings came into my head, no doubt about lightbulbs and snakes and jelly beans and tractors or some other idiocy.

Instead, what I remembered was that first time I was in love. The girl left me for another boy, and I was destroyed.

My father came out to where I was sniffling down by the creek behind our house. He stood before me, and when I looked up, he slapped me hard in the face.

Slapped me so hard that I fell off the log onto my back.

He said: "That's all it is, Boone. That hurt. It may even be black and blue, you might have a black eye. But all I did was what the girl did to you. That hit to the face won't kill you, and neither will having your heart broken. It happens, and it heals, and you'll be better for it. I know you'll have a hard time believing that, but it's true. You have to roll with the punches, you have no other choice, we all have to, not just you, and you're not singled out, no reason to feel sorry for yourself. So as you look at the bruise each day in the mirror, and you watch it go away, let your heart heal, too. You have lots of people who love you, boy. Me, your Mom, sister Crocket, all your aunts and uncles and gramps. Hold us close, and heal. There will be other women, and you'll have your heart broken again someday. That's just the way it is."

I scrambled to my feet, sobbing, and hugged him.

It was the only time he ever, *ever* cut the crap and gave it to me straight

And right when I needed it most.

Or perhaps I needed it most as I knelt in that fetid jungle with a rifle barrel under my chin.

I stood and heaved a sigh, my eyes bloodshot from anguish and my insides full of snakes and jellybeans. Or lightbulbs and tractors. Whatever was going on in there, it was as if I was being eaten from the inside out. But that feeling would only get worse if those pirates caught up with me. The day had started badly enough, but there was a shot that I could be rescued and start the process of watching my bruises fade.

More importantly, I had to tap anger rather than heartbreak. The whole reason I was in this situation was because I had been manipulated. They blew up King Max to try to force me to become His Majesty, and when that didn't work, they inadvertently stuck me on Toad Caye, heartbroken and fighting for my life. My life? My fate.

Fighting for control of my fate.

To blast off the top of my skull in that lowly state would be to let those who had put me there win.

As with the striped marlin, you win the day by not

blowing it when you are utterly drained and wondering why you have to continue.

I heard a shout echo from over where my camp was, and I nimbly retraced the path back to the rock face and climbed to the top of the toad, crouching. Peering through the trees, I still saw no one on the beach, but I heard other shouting. And then I heard what sounded like men talking in my camp. Perhaps some of my booby traps went off – to good effect? They wouldn't kill anybody, but they might break an arm or collar bone.

I needed to know how many of them there were.

Scuttling to one side, I jockeyed my eye to look through the trees toward the frigate. Sophie and the Zodiac were bearing down on the frigate, and no pirates were in her wake. So at least I had accomplished something. One of us was rescued.

Could I just hide until the French landed?

That would be too risky. Were I discovered, that would be it. I had to keep moving where they had just been, if I could figure out how.

Yet in my time anticipating the arrival of pirates, I had conceived of a plan, a trap as it were. Now, in the clutches, did I dare try to pull it off?

I was terrified it would fail.

Three rounds of ammunition was all I had, and I was not any kind of marksman, certainly not with a strange weapon. To use it effectively, I would have to do so in close range, and my plan allowed for that. I had originally anticipated executing it with my cross bow.

Picking my way down and around to the lea side of the island, I kept a sharp ear as I approached the rock outcrop just around the corner from the tiger trap, the starting point of my strategy.

I peered around the corner, and saw the path to the trap meandering off into the woods. I could hear the voices louder than before up on the ledge where the camp was.

Anybody coming down the trail from the camp would see the path toward where I was.

"I'm injured!" I shouted.

Voices, and then footfalls.

I backed around the corner, my weapon ready.

In the distance I could see Sophie had reached the frigate, and that landing boats were being lowered next to the ship.

Dawn was making the overcast sky pink, clouds rippled like folds in a bedsheet.

Footsteps.

CRACK! CRASH!

Shouts.

I shouldered my weapon and stepped out from behind the rock.

Six lean black men stood thirty feet away staring down into the collapsed tiger pit between us, and a seventh below them was yelling and screaming.

I shot one of the six in the chest, but hit another in the shoulder. The former staggered back, dropped his weapon and fell to his side, squirming. The other fell to his knees, gripping his shoulder.

The rest, including Freddie, shouldered their weapons and fired. But not before I had dashed back around the corner and made tracks through the jungle.

In the time it took them to get around the pit and give chase I was just far enough that their bullets missed the mark or were intercepted by branches. But they followed, which was what I wanted. I knew every foot of that forest and was far faster making my way over to the other side.

And of course I had arranged some of those finger conchs and vines strategically as stumbling and tripping hazards, all buried just under the leaf litter. I knew where to hop over them, and to run with my feet high.

One of them shouted: "We need him alive!"

I hoped there were not more pirates when I emerged on the opposite side of the island, at the beach where I thought their boats might be. If so, my goose was cooked.

Then again, if they did shoot me, it would do what I had not when I knelt with the rifle barrel under my chin. I did not relish looking in the mirror and watching my bruises fade. My soul was weary, and it took every bit of my father's slap in the face twenty years prior to sustain me.

I raced through the jungle where the bats were just returning to roost, their leathery wings crashing through the canopy. Right then, they took the opportunity to relieve themselves, no doubt their bowels heavy with fruit from the night's feast. It was an actual shit storm, and I veered to have my pursuers pass directly through the worst of it. Indeed, I took some hits, but nothing like what those behind me encountered as hundreds of bats burst into the canopy and promptly spewed a long jet of foul slime below.

I heard shouts and curses behind me as they tripped and stumbled and were splattered with guano.

I drew near the edge of the forest, and could see the pirates' boats on the beach. A much younger pirate, a kid, was standing by the boats. The men behind me began to yell at him to stop me.

Fumbling with a rifle that looked too big for him, the kid ran toward me as I approached the beach.

Killing a twelve year old child gave me obvious pause, even one trying to shoot me.

When he saw my approach, he shouldered his rifle. He was too far from me to risk my last round of ammo, so I dropped to the ground when he fired in full auto over my head.

The barrel flashed with a rapid succession of cracks, leaves and branches shredding above me.

The boy lost control of the rifle in full auto, the recoil forcing the aim higher and higher toward the sky before the magazine was suddenly empty. A standard magazine on most submachine guns lasts only three seconds in full auto. My pursuers screamed, protesting and cursing – in firing over my head, the kid had fired directly at them.

Wide-eyed, the boy pirate merely watched as I

jumped to my feet and angled along the edge of the jungle back toward camp. I could only hope the kid had accidentally shot a few of his mates and reduced the number of my pursuers.

I came full circle, back to the path up to camp, and I remembered that the one pirate I shot in the chest by the tiger pit dropped his rifle. The other was only shot in the shoulder. Should I risk the tiger pit and hope I could secure another weapon? One or both of theirs?

Gingerly, but out of breath and gasping, I took a look down the path, and I could see both men on their backs and not moving.

I drew my sword and raced in.

Shoulder Man jerked upright, fumbling with his gun with one hand, but I reached him first and cut him down across the neck, blood spraying all over me. I kicked him aside, pulled his weapon away, and then knelt to pick up Chest's.

No time.

Running footsteps approached from around the corner of the path behind me.

I swung Shoulder's weapon and fired with one arm toward the footsteps. The gun was on full auto, so I could not control my aim any better than the twelve year old boy on the beach, the muzzle rising, but I knew enough to fire short bursts.

Three pirates came into view and dove for the ground.

I dropped the empty weapon and sprinted up the

path to my camp, bullets humming past my head.

My remaining rifle had one round left, and as I dashed into my camp I cast it aside the propane tanks mounted behind my little fortification.

I seized the sparker, turned a nob and lit the pilot light.

Water bottles filled with gasoline were in a row next to the tanks, and I began flicking off the tops and tossing them over my rock pile rampart. I heard them smack into trees, spraying their contents as they fell to the forest floor.

Footfalls came up the trail.

Cranking the burners, I shot propane flames down the path.

In seconds, the forest before me erupted with Hades fury. A wall of roaring fire rose abruptly before me, hot enough that I had to retreat from my flamethrower toward the sulfur bath and rock face.

A pirate leapt from the flames into my camp and rolled on the ground, the flames engulfing him quickly extinguished.

On his feet in an instant, his eyes locked onto where I stood against the rock face.

It was none other than Freddie, the shaven pirate with the broken flat nose, the one who I shot in the leg. His clothes smoking, his hair singed, his face sooty, he trained his rifle on me.

His grimace told me he no longer cared about ransom, only murder, and revenge.

Spiteful eyes under smoldering eyebrows beheld me with bloodlust.

Surrender was not an option, only submission to oblivion.

My weapon with the last round was back next to the fuel tanks, near him.

All I had was my sword.

The sword that had started out as a ceremonial sword but had turned into an invaluable tool for survival.

But it was no match for a rifle.

Ah, well. In that moment, I was resigned, and almost glad that I wouldn't have to endure being rescued, parting from Sophie, dealing with Zarenga Chi, Putin, publicity, movie rights, talk shows...I could just die a shabby man in my island hovel and finally rest, no longer kismet's punching bag.

Incomprehensibly, there was an arrow sticking out of Freddie's neck.

And then another.

The smoldering pirate began to jerk violently fumbling at the arrows...dropping his weapon.

Another arrow protruded from his chest.

I had been looking at the fulcrum of my demise so intently that my peripheral vision failed to detect Sophie, who had slipped around the corner from the back way over the rocks. Emerging behind the pirate, she had snatched up the crossbow and quiver. The tumult and crackle of the forest fire overwhelmed any sound of her entrance.

That darling French lassie had returned with the French soldiers. As I learned later, she had insisted on guiding them back to save me. When they insisted otherwise, she remained in the Zodiac and turned back to the island.

They followed.

Crossbow at her side, and tears streaming down her cheeks, Sophie looked in horror at the pirate squirming on the ground at her feet.

I stepped forward smartly, my sword singing as it left its scabbard, and I plunged the blade into the poor bastard's chest.

More killing. More waste. More blood.

A French sailor in camouflage, helmet and tactical gear turned the corner from where Sophie came in, his weapon at the ready, his eyes taking in the scene. She was much more nimble than he, and she knew the way so was faster, making her appearance sooner.

And just in time.

The soldier didn't know me from Adam, and so targeted his red laser sight on my chest.

I raised my hands and dropped my sword. Wouldn't do to have gone through all that only to be gunned down accidentally, would it?

Smoke billowed from the jungle, smelling like burnt coffee and autumnal leaf piles – someone was speaking French from a bullhorn down on the beach, demanding surrender.

Sophie fell to her knees sobbing, soot and ash

swirling through what once was our whole existence.

An existence virtually and literally up in flames.

Our lounge chairs, the ones in which we would sip brandy and watch the sunset and listen to Sophie sing her catalogue of plants – aflame.

In a moment, the tarp would alight, the water bottles would shrivel from the heat, and the sulfur pool would fill with cinders.

Everything up in smoke.

CHAPTER 25

NOT ONCE DID I LOOK BACK AS I LEFT TOAD CAYE.

After an examination and bandaging of all my scrapes and scratches by the ship's doctor, and a tepid but most welcome shower, the crew scrounged up a grey jumpsuit that I traded for my rags. I made it clear that I wanted to retain them, my sword and the bent, rusty cross of valor. The silver capsule with the thumb drive never left my neck.

Summarily, I was led by a swabbie to a poop deck where there were two benches and a picnic table bolted to the deck, the steely sea all around under leaden skies. It was not raining, and it was sultry.

At the table sat the captain in khakis, his hat on the table, and large striped captain's epaulettes. He stood as I approached, and extended a hand, gesturing with the other for me to sit down. Heavy and active eyebrows, grey with years, sat above perceptive hazel eyes bracketing a Roman nose, his silvering hair close cropped with a razor straight part on one side.

He spoke in heavily accented, halting English.

"I can only think, Mr. Linsenbigler, that by reputation, you could use a drink?" From beside him he hefted a large tumbler of ice graced with a brown liquid, and set it before me.

I cleared my throat, and said hoarsely: "That and the rest of the bottle, and case, if you please." The strength of the liquor caught me by surprise – my guess that the figgy, citrusy whiskey was some sort of blended scotch like Grants. I suppressed a wheeze as it went down. He continued.

"We have notified both the Zarengi and American embassies in Madagascar that we are bringing you there. How do you feel? The doctor says that you seem in good health. It has been, what, almost a year that you went missing, presumed dead?"

I sipped and laughed grimly. "*Presumed dead.* Might as well just change my name to that at this juncture. P.D. Linsenbigler, at your service."

He squinted as he followed my English with effort. Then, with hands clasped behind his back, he turned away to survey the sea. "You know, you are not my first castaway."

The liquor settled into me like an old dog into its bed, and I heaved a great sigh and said nothing. He continued, facing away.

"I was stranded on an atoll to the southeast of Madagascar for six months. Our patrol boat hit a monsoon squall. Some poor decisions led to us going down. I managed to cling to the hull. The others did not. The reef made quick work of the boat, and I swam to shore. The rest…well, you know the rest. You make it your business to survive, all the while the horizon full of false promise." He turned, his brow knit. "I know what you've been through."

"I'd hazard to guess ours is a rather exclusive club, Captain."

He picked up my drink and took a sip, placing it back in front of me. "Of course, now your time on the island is behind you. Or is it?"

Inwardly I shook my head – I'd forgotten about how people converse so obliquely.

He tossed his head toward the stern. "What I am saying, Linsenbigler, is that returning will not be simple, either. Do not get lost in the bottle. I did. There's no future there."

Rolling the tumbler between my hands, I admired the golden brown liquid and twinkling, alien iciness of the cubes within. "Captain, believe me, I have very definite plans for my return, and I'm quite clear where I need to end up and what my goals are going forward. There will be no time for self-pity."

He put a foot on the bench next to me, and leaned in with an elbow on his knee, tossing his head again. "I see. And what of the girl, Sophie?"

My gut tightened, and I could see in his face that he saw my pain.

"We survived, together. And that's it."

He put a hand on my shoulder, his eyes inspecting mine, and it made me want to let it all go, part the skies and rain.

But no. Maybe sometime else, by myself, but not then, I needed to remain strong and put all that aside, behind. I needed to hold the hard slap to my face near and dear. Time to move forward, no backtracking. To do that would be to let those people who manipulated me win. And I was determined that it was I that would come out on top and take control of my destiny.

Or die trying.

If my time on that godforsaken rock would have meaning or value, have any redeeming merit whatsoever, I had to stay vigilant, as if boating a marlin.

He added. "We wired her husband. She's in rough shape, and we had to sedate her."

"Well, it isn't every day you shoot a man in the throat with a crossbow, so I can see why she's distraught. You have to get used to killing people. I have. Not that I ever wanted to, but there you have it. Let me see…there were seven pirates, and I'm not sure how many are just maimed, but I killed a fistful. Was glad not to kill the child. Add that to the one I killed the first time they came and that's likely six. Add that to those I killed in Russia. Three in the helicopter, and one other, though that was sort of an accident. In the Caribbean I lanced two men to death. So unless I've forgotten one – I have! The Mongolian bandit, so all together, let's see…why that's thirteen men I've slaughtered! Fancy that."

I wiped an errant tear from my cheek.

Thirteen. A Fibonacci number.

The captain stepped away, hands clasped behind his back again, nodding. "It is all well and good to be strong, Linsenbigler. But that can get the better of you, too."

"I appreciate the insight," I said bitterly, not meaning a word of it. It was too soon to hear all this. "What month is this?"

"March."

I nodded, breathing deeply. Ten Months. At this time the previous year I was likely in Istanbul recovering from the previous imbroglio. That didn't hold a candle to this one. "Can I request that you reach out to my publicist Terry Orbach at Orbach Productions and inform him that I will be in Madagascar in...?"

"Day after tomorrow we dock in Toamasina. We have to finish our patrol."

"Tell him I'll be there on Sunday and that he should prepare his film crews and provide me with transportation to Zarenga Chi – but not sponsored by them. I am, shall we say, done with government transport and will rely on only that of my own arrangement."

He pursed his lips, nodding. "No message to your family?"

"My sister will read about it in the paper, like last time. Oh, and if you would, please inform Terry and the Zarengi consulate in Madagascar that I will consent to ascendancy to His Majesty of Zarenga Chi as long as I am released from my contract with Amalgamated

Consumables upon my coronation. Or I can do all this myself if I'm set in front of a laptop with connectivity."

His eyes widened. "Are you aware of the turn of events in Zarenga Chi? The King's Council declared you dead. The council is struggling to take control amid general labor strikes and protests. They've deployed troops. The people are demanding open elections. They want an independent investigation of the assassination of Maximillian and of your disappearance."

I managed a weary smile, helped by the whiskey. "Could I make anything worse by being their king?"

"Yes, you might. You really should give this further thought now that you're off that island, give it a little time."

I finished the glass of whiskey in a mighty gulp.

"I've already done my share of thinking on this, all the time I need. And if my stay on Toad Caye has had influence on how I think, likely it's all for better, not worse. Perhaps your incarceration on your island was under different circumstance from mine. If being marooned was all about survival, then those lessons are complimentarily transferrable to those in Zarenga Chi, where I should have spent less time eyeing the horizon and more on what was around me, and what's in it for me. Sometimes you have to do what's best for others to do what's best for yourself, and if that means self-sacrifice, then, as my father would say, you've got asparagus in your socks. The trick of course, you know, or may not, it's not here or there, is you have to tet your strap and then spring it if you want to pool the firates."

"Mr. Linsenbigler, I believe you're drunk."

"Indeed, and I thank you for that. It was a tong lime coming."

CHAPTER 26

MY CORONATION WAS AT THE LICHTENBICHLER PALACE BY THE SEA.

Palace after a fashion, of course. More like a sprawling white Victorian mansion, replete with turrets, archways, dormers and intricate gables. The roof was red tile and had a Moorish flavor to it. The approach from the front of the mansion passed through a row of soaring palms ending in a large circular driveway at the palace entrance, a fountain in the center made from the shells of a hundred and one giant clams. Lawns rolled away to either side dotted with clusters of fancy tropical plants overflowing with lush, purple flowers, peacocks strutting to and fro.

At the back of the palace, a great lawn stretched a long city block down to the sea and a narrow beach, flanked on both sides by volcanic outcrops topped by old black powder cannons pointed out to sea.

A wide stage had been erected at the back of the palace and attached to the back porch, the highest point of which was an upper deck and promontory where Maximillian von Lichtenbichler the First used to host lawn parties for his people.

Stairs down the center of this promontory landed on a wider, lower porch. Rows of chairs had been arranged facing the upper deck where I would make my acceptance speech. These chairs were for the King's Council and foreign dignitaries.

A stairway down from the center of the lower porch landed at the stage where a military orchestra was arrayed, their white uniforms starched and their pith helmets festooned with plumes of white and black booby feathers.

Just on the other side of the orchestra, and a step or two down, the press was a jagged line of cameras on tripods, crouching photographers, and techies with recording equipment.

The press flanked yet another stair down to the lawn itself – where there were more chairs for lesser dignitaries. Beyond that was a military unit, arms at the ready, separating the stage from the loyal subjects, who stretched all the way down to the beach, their blue eyes all trained on Boone von Lichtenbichler the First as he stepped onto the promontory deck, hulking halfback palace guards flanking my rear.

An hour earlier, I had been at another ceremony of much pomp at the Nambia Lutheran Church where I was blessed and suitably vetted before God for my ascension. I passed with flying colors, somehow. Well, if God didn't want me there, didn't want me a king, he had had plenty of opportunities to intercede, which gave me half an inkling that this is what He had been angling at all along, the wily bastard.

Of course, the month leading up to this hallowed day was spent first in negotiations with my lawyer Bubby Hecklin (I had him flown in) and the King's Council and the political representatives of the ZLF. Everybody had to be satisfied with this arrangement, of reinstating the monarchy, to keep the peace. One interesting codicil of my new 'contract' was that as His Majesty, I was committed to siring heirs, a task to which I thought I could aspire quite nicely. All I would need was a 'queen dowager' – that means she has no power. Interesting stuff I never knew about Royals. Anywho, they wanted to make sure they had as many heirs as possible so that this sort of crisis would not reoccur.

I felt a little sorry for the ZLF. They had been bargained down to representation by non-binding referendums on 'critical matters of state.' Bargained down? Something told me the ZLF representatives had been bribed into over compromising.

The crux of the negotiations was really that I would be a compliant king who would mollify the public and not sulk and plot like Max III.

Through all of this, I never once mentioned anything about the assassination attempt of Ol' Boonie over Mumu's lava pit, or about Russians or Putin or any of that. I said the balloon pilot lost his balance when Max III was dropped and fell overboard. Not very convincing, but it didn't need to be, my handlers likely knew I was lying anyway. As I have said before, to mingle with these types of people, you have to cling to knowing something they don't, or letting them think they know something you don't know, or have them think something that you know that you don't. Is that clear? I didn't think so. It's all about playing your cards close to the vest, bluffing, and keeping your poker face.

I made it clear that I'd had plenty of time to think it over, and that after my experiences on Toad Caye, all I wanted was to spend the rest of my days at leisure with plenty of booze and fully-staffed fishing boat. If being king and keeping the peace and being a phony was what they wanted me to do…well, wasn't that who I was anyway? Everybody knew I was just an actor, so why pass up this plum gig in a giant palace by the sea? And why would I, as an actor, even attempt to govern or meddle in matters that I did not understand, much less risk ending up on Vladimir Putin's hit list? Give me that queen consort and I'll impregnate the daylights out of her, then let the nannies raise the brats while I'm tangling with wahoo in the briny blue.

Really, though – why the hell not pick the low hanging bongos? Wasn't that what I did when I originally signed on as a liquor pitchman for Conglomerated Beverages? Wasn't that my deal with their CEO devil, Prentis Hargreaves?

Linus sat below as a dignitary, beaming up at me like Dr. Frankenstein admiring his handiwork. He sat with the

U.S. Ambassador to Madagascar and the Comoros, the King's Council and rock-like Kinkaid front and center. All were dressed in black tie, white gloves and tails and looking akin to the proverbial cats who swallowed an entire flock of canaries. Or perhaps boobies.

And His Majesty was decked out much as I had been on my fated balloon flight, except I had my ceremonial sword across my back, ninja style. Far superior placement, as I had learned the hard way and firsthand.

Atop my head was the larger colonial-type pith helmet, in white, with a jaunty purple plume.

On my breast plate was the beat-up Cross of Valor, layered with another medallion, that of the royal twin-palms and crown of His Royal Highness. Solid gold.

Likely, nobody back in Ho-Ho-Kus, New Jersey ever thought I had this in me. Had that bully Ted Van Peebles known I was destined to this, he might well not have punched my arm black and blue back at elementary school. And that tart who broke my heart, Hester Moutard? You blew it, honey. You could have been Queen Dowager instead of a clerk at the Lodi Motor Vehicle Commission – had you played your cards right.

The military band thumped out the national anthem, an oopmah number, and the crowd sang along, albeit with less vigor than when I made my balloon ascent. I sensed tension – a lot had passed by the board since I'd soared off into oblivion, and suspicion and cynicism were the coin of the realm.

So as I stepped through the purple velvet curtains onto the promontory, about to become monarch, was there no thought of Sophie? Was that all behind me?

There was thought of her, and my time on the island, but not of the heartache, which was still there, and would be for a very long time. Dealing with that was for another time, as I said, and I had managed to hold that course over the last month. I only caught a glimpse of her one last time when we disembarked the French frigate. Our eyes did not meet. Just as well.

A cluster of silver microphones was at the dais, and I stopped in front of them, gazing across the expanse of dignitaries and schemers, musicians and sensationalizers, soldiers and citizens.

All at once the Drum Major dropped his mace and the music stopped.

Throats were cleared, and the audience settled into their chairs, and adjusted their stance, ready to hear what I had to say.

I placed my prepared remarks, those vetted by the Kings Council and Bubby Hecklin, face down on the dais.

"My father, Eustace Peter Linsenbigler, was a man of few and often strange words." The words echoed out over the great lawn, gulls and frigate birds soaring over the ocean blue.

The Kings Council all shifted uncomfortably in their seats. I glanced at Trimble and witnessed his grin fade. My father was not part of the script.

"For example, on an occasion such as this, he would likely tell me: *Son, you can only bottle so many peaches before the sump pump fails.*"

I smiled and paused. A chuckle trickled from the citizenry. Alas, not Kinkaid or his crew.

I waved a hand across my assembled subjects: "I will leave it to you to interpret that as you will."

Another laugh – always good to open with a joke, *n'est pas?*

I went back to script, but left the paper in front of me face down.

"I, Boone Linsenbigler, great grandson of His Late Majesty Maximillian von Lichtenbichler, accept his name and his mantle. As such, I, Boone von Lichtenbichler, humbly accept and embrace my duty to Zarenga Chi and its subjects, and accept and embrace my ascendancy to your Royal Majesty, King of Zarenga Chi!" I threw out my arms dramatically, and the crowd roared, the Kings Council on their feet, a look of relief on their faces that I was back on script. Trimble had indulged his Cheshire cat smile again.

When the applause died, and seats were retaken, I surveyed those assembled with gravity, my chin high.

"How may I best serve my country, my subjects, one and all? You know, when I was marooned on that island, all I thought about was survival."

The King's Council was once again agape, and Trimble was frowning. *Off script.*

"I was alone, at first, and I became good fending for myself, good at finding food and water and innovating to make shelter and protect myself from pirates. Yet, living that way, living only to provide for myself, was a hollow experience. Zarenga Chi prides itself on providing for all – as any nation as wealthy as this one should. Which is why when a woman was stranded with me on that island, I found renewed purpose in fending for her, and she found renewed purpose in helping me endure the ordeal of isolation and privation. We endured together, equally, and when I sacrificed for her by staying behind to fend off the pirates, she would not abandon me. At the risk of her own life, she returned and saved your King's life."

I paused, and all I could hear were the waves crashing on the rocks.

"It would be easy for me to be your king and abandon you to the status quo, to the pirates."

I glanced at Trimble. His mouth was agape with horror, his nose wrinkled, his glasses lightly steamed. Anytime you put that expression on the face of a manipulator like him, you know you're doing the right thing.

"But if my life was saved for a reason, let it be for this decree, one that I am fully empowered to make in conformance with the Codicils of the Realm. As your Majesty, King of Zarenga Chi, I decree that henceforth this nation will be a parliamentary democracy, with elections to be held within the year. At such time the elections are held, monitored and validated by representatives of the United Nations, and parliament is established and a democracy recognized to the satisfaction of that international body, I will cede my authority to rule and will retire…"

I didn't have a chance to finish.

Well, had I attempted to, nobody would have heard me.

Several things happened below me right at the end of my decree.

Kinkaid leapt from his seat and assaulted the sound technician tucked under the promontory to try to silence the mics.

The rest of the stuffy white and Asian men in the King's Council jumped to their feet and began shouting protestations at me, fists in the air.

Trimble headed for the exit, full steam ahead, the cat disappearing with his smile.

The press corps surged forward into the band, snapping photos furiously, camera flashes rapid fire.

Most importantly, the spectators, the Zarengi natives, erupted in a cheer that likely was heard as far away as Madagascar.

I would like to think that, just maybe, an echo of that cheer reached Toad Caye, drifting through the burned forest across the cinders of my shambled camp, and into the sharp ears of the roosting fruit bats, now safe from my darts.

Like a quarterback going for it on fourth down, one score behind, and ten seconds on the clock, I turned to the Royal Guard. The giant black men grinned at me, and were clapping their large hands with slow, deliberate approval of my decree.

"Gentlemen?" I waved them toward me into a huddle. "I need you to escort me down there, through the crowd and to the beach. Can you do that?"

They said nothing, just exchanged glances and prepared a flying wedge formation at the head of the stair.

When we reached the landing, I could see between the hulking Royal Guards that the members of the Kings Council were shouting at those off the stage toward the troops.

At the next landing, the royal guard pushed through the band and paused as the press crew scattered before them on the next stair. I locked eyes with the Drum Major and pointed a commanding finger. "Play, damn you!"

As we started down the next steps to the lawn, drums thumped and the tubas honked, the Zarengi oompah anthem pounding out over the cheers of the masses below.

At the bottom step, on terra firma, we stopped.

My guards turned in and looked at me for our next move, parting so that I could see that the military was no longer facing the crowd.

They were facing us.

Rifles shouldered.

Aimed at me.

*Well, Boonie, you upstart knucklehead, look where it all ends!
It was a nice try, though, and you can finally die now, and with no
regrets.*

Then, all at once the soldiers stumbled backward,
some rifles firing into the air as they fell.

My Zarengi subjects had latched onto the soldiers
and pulled them back, collapsing their ranks and surging
forward and around us.

I pulled my sword, and held it high, shouting: "To
the beach!"

Moses himself would have popped a vest button
with pride as the sea of Zarengis parted before me, a
deafening chant rumbling through my subjects.

BOONE! BOONE! BOONE!

The band pounded out the national anthem, and I
marched in time to the beat of the drums.

Heady stuff, and I daresay, in that moment I had
second thoughts about leaving ol' ZC. For once I was
being cheered for something I actually did, and was
worthy of being cheered.

In that moment, I was no longer the liquor company
shill and phony hero.

In that moment, I actually was a hero.

Terry's timing was impeccable. As the crowd parted
and the beach appeared, so did the chartered seaplane
angling in toward the beach across the surface of the bay.

Not just any seaplane, but an Antilles Super Goose,
which has a boat body instead of pontoons, and a long
upper wing mounted with twin turboprop engines. It can

go about 230 miles per hour, and has a range of 1300 miles – enough to easily reach the Malagasy town of Antsiranana for refueling, and from there an easy two-hour hop to the French territory island of Mayotte, where I would get a commercial flight to Paris and beyond.

The Super Goose is one of the fastest seaplanes, and the idea behind chartering one was to get as far away as possible as soon as possible. I had no idea how far the Russians would go to punish someone like me who had defied their will. Would they go so far as to send MiGs to shoot down our Super Goose? Killing me now would look awfully suspicious, but when did Putin ever care about looking suspicious? He has brazenly poisoned and assassinated defectors, investigative reporters and dissidents in other countries, and even right in front of the Kremlin.

One thing was for sure – Boone von Lichtenbichler wasn't safe in his kingdom and would be compelled to live in a self-imposed exile.

And once the Times printed their Putin money laundering story the following morning, the one based on that thumb drive, my life wouldn't be worth two red pennies.

Not if it weren't for Bubby. He was issuing a letter on behalf of yours truly to the Russian Embassy claiming that there were two thumb drives. The other...well, let's just call it an insurance policy. Anything happens to ol' Boone, and, well, that second one will go to the Times, too. What's on that one? Care to find out?

I didn't think so.

The plane spun and angled its tail toward shore, ready to launch back out over the sea, engines roaring.

Turning to the crowd, I raised my sword, then placed it across my chest and bowed so deeply my helmet almost fell off.

And when I came upright again, Tanya stepped from the throng.

She was not in the suit, sunglasses and earpiece uniform of a security agent but in cargo pants, tactical sandals and red sun hoodie, a rucksack slung over her shoulder. Her short blond hair was tousled the way she used to wear it.

She stepped up to me, and over the din of the cheering crowds she said: "I wasn't really sorry when I wrote you that note." Her lavender eyes searched mine. "Not like I am now. I thought I was doing the right thing for the right reasons for the right people. We put Foresh up to getting that drive as a service to her country, and we found all the other thumb drives. But you knew all this, or figured it out?"

I shrugged. *Of course.*

Behind me I heard the plane door open, and Terry shout: "Boone! Come on!"

She looked down, and then back at me. "I had no business getting involved in this, or betraying you, not after what you did for me back in the Bahamas. And when they tried to kill you in that balloon, when we didn't release the Putin documents on the thumb drives...I want you to know my job-first attitude was a mistake, that I'm not willing to commit to a job where I don't know for sure who the good guys are. So I've resigned from the government, from my job. Boone, you and I are on different paths that keep crossing, but my path needs to veer off in a different direction from where it was going. I'm not asking you to forgive me, I just want you to understand. And that I am sorry that I betrayed you."

She began to back up.

"Boone!" Terry shouted.

"Fair enough, Tanya, but you'll never get where you're going that direction. They won't let you quit. Likely they won't let you live." I jerked a thumb over my shoulder at the plane. "As a friend, I'm offering you a ride. Not as a lover, just a friend. Our path forward is as friends."

She blinked at me, hesitating.

"Boone!" Terry shrieked.

"Come on, Tanya, Tabitha or Tamara, whatever your name is." I grinned, teasing about her many aliases. "Let's have a cocktail and fly out of this loony bin."

I turned and marched right into the water toward the open door of the Super Goose where the co-pilot and Terry stood beckoning. I grabbed the co-pilot's hand, and he hoisted me up out of the water and into the doorway of the vibrating plane.

When I turned Tamara had not followed.

She had vanished into the crowd, unable to accept help from the man she betrayed. *Damn.* Another unfortunate goodbye.

So be it. Perhaps our paths would cross again if she got out of there alive.

Standing majestically in the plane's doorway, my final gesture to the crowd was my patented Roman salute: *Hail, Caesar!*

I stepped back and the co-pilot yanked the door closed with a decisive *whump.*

The cabin had four leather lounge chairs, two facing forward and two aft. The aft seats contained Terry and a cameraman.

The fore seats were empty, and the bar was next to that, no mere coincidence.

I looked back out the porthole in the door at the crowd as the growl of the engines soared. The Zarengi natives had overrun all the palace balconies, and were waving the royal crossed palm flags, the oompah music still faintly audible over the engines.

I turned to the camera, smoothed my mustache, and said: "Looks as if my work is done here in Zarenga Chi!"

"CUT!" Terry shouted. "Boone, that's not the line!"

"It's not?"

"No, the line is: *My work here in Zarenga Chi is done.*"

I rolled my eyes. "What's the difference?"

"The line is the line! OK, once more. Camera rolling? And...action!"

I brandished my sword, twirled it and deftly slid it into the scabbard on my back with a *schwing*.

Raising an eyebrow at the camera, I announced: "My work in Zarenga Chis is done, *for now*. What better time for a cocktail!" I tossed my helmet on the floor and began unbuttoning my tunic.

"Cut! Boone…"

"And print, cameraman. That's the final take! It's a wrap!"

The plane surged forward, lift off imminent.

Moments later, icy cocktail tinkling in my glass, Terry sulking across from me like a child who wants a pony, the plane circled the Lichtenbichler Palace by the sea, and I gazed back down on the ecstatic mob blanketing the grounds, back down on Zarenga Chi.

Then I leaned back in my comfy seat, closed my eyes and heaved a sigh.

I toasted that little troubled island, Sophie and Tanya.

Adieu.

EPILOGUE

FIFTY-SEVEN SATURDAYS LATER, MR. PRENTIS HARGREAVES WAS AT MY DOOR.

Last time, I was summoned to him and he dispensed me to Africa.

Now he came to me.

I was not in New York, but in a tropical location that I will not publicly disclose except to say that it is one of the premier locations for wahoo angling. I had boated four. Sixteen had either cut me off, thrown the hook or lined me.

So Prentis had come all the way from New York to talk to me. Personally. It was not wholly unexpected as Bubby Hecklin had heard from Conglomerated Beverages that they were interested in re-signing me, to which I replied, simply, "Ha."

Likewise, I was alerted to his visit the night before when he arrived at the airport. It pays to have scouts at the airport.

My simple white bungalow was on stilts in a grove of

thick palms, oceanside, while my dock and skiff were on the other side of the island, bayside.

Prentis stood at the top of the stairs looking out at the ocean, the breeze ruffling the silver racing stripes in his hair. As one might imagine, he was in khakis, with a white button-down shirt and blue blazer sporting the crest of his yacht club. He almost seemed surprised to see me when I opened the door, or perhaps just surprised that I was so underdressed by comparison. My floral pink Hawaiian shirt hung open over my fishing shorts, feet bare, my hair in a wild mane and my whiskers in top, flowing condition.

This was a different kind of feral Boone – outwardly the one with the Drifters Reef bar walking distance, who only cared about fishing, cocktails and, at the moment, Brandi, who appeared next to me.

A ravishing, tanned blonde, Brandi was a twenty-something barmaid at 'The Reef.' She wrinkled her nose at Prentis, before kissing me on the cheek.

"See you at The Reef, Boonie. Remember: you promised to show everybody that new drink. Everybody loves the new bitters."

I patted her bikinied bottom in response, and without a second glance at Prentis, she slid past us and bounced down the stair, all the while slipping on a white floral beach jacket over her lovely torso.

Prentis eyed Brandi's departure, then me. "Not interrupting anything, I hope?"

I smirked, stepping back into the bungalow. "Come

in, Prentis. I'm of course surprised to see you here..."

He had the air of a father walking into his teenage son's bedroom – aghast at the décor. One wall next to a window was all fly rods floor to ceiling racked horizontally. Opposite that was the kitchen, which was dominated by what looked like one of those chemistry sets you see in old movies, large beakers and tubes running this way and that. Shoved in to one side of the sink were thirty or forty bottles of liquor. Wedged into the kitchen under the counter was an ice machine, which took the opportunity to break the silence with a crash of fresh cubes.

Beyond was the open door to my bedroom, rack full of tropical shirts next to an unmade bed.

Coffee table: strewn with fly reels, fly boxes and cigar boxes.

Sofa: dotted with fishing magazines and a sole pair of striped panties.

My fly tying table in the corner was a jumble of craft fur, synthetic hair, tinsel and flash material atop stray boxes of stainless steel hooks and thread bobbins.

A patina of rust graced my sword, which was propped in the corner by the door.

From under his arm, Prentis produced a bottle of bourbon. He cocked an eyebrow and held it out to me. "They said you'd probably appreciate some bourbon. Thought we might have a drink and talk."

I took the bottle and eyed the label. Indeed, one could not find the likes of it anywhere near my hideaway, and I immediately cracked the seal. "Why not?"

I searched and found two relatively clean tumblers, charged them with ice, and filled them with lovely golden-brown bourbon. "Let's sit on the veranda, Prentis, things are kind of a jumble in here, maid's day off as they say."

He glanced with suppressed dismay over the jumble, tacitly agreeing, and I unfolded a couple cheap lawn chairs for us to sit on at the landing at the top of the stairs. I dragged a faded blue cooler over for a table between us to put our drinks on, and grabbed a bag of chili-cheese corn chips, which I split and splayed. *Hors d'oeuvres*, at the ready!

I broke the ice. "I hope you didn't come all this way just to see me?"

"And if I did?"

"I'm flattered, of course, though…"

He squinted at me. "So you're no longer a king?"

"Not as of last week. The UN cajoled them to form a parliament, and the World Bank helped the central bank disengage from the money laundering. A lot of loose ends, of course, but I have formally abdicated." I spread my arms. "You behold the late, great king of Zarenga Chi, slayer of pirates and master volcano balloonist!"

He sipped his drink, squinting at me, crow's feet splayed back from his steel blue eyes. "And in some rarified circles, they say you're responsible for release of the Nambia Papers, and slayer of Vladimir Putin's money laundering operation."

"Do they, now?" I squinted back at him. "I see my

reputation has rebounded beyond any reason."

He stood, gazing out at the sunlight twinkling on the ocean, waves crashing, magpies whistling.

"You know we want you back at Conglomerated."

"Yes, I've noted that the stock hasn't held up all that well, recently. But why am I all of a sudden a viable commodity? After all, I thought…"

"No sense throwing my words back at me, Mr. Linsenbigler. At the time, selling your contract was the right decision for our shareholders. Things have changed since then."

"Have they? For whom?"

"Keeping things in perspective, let us not forget your humble beginnings, and Conglomerated's part in elevating your station."

I snorted. "Well, that did have something to do with my bitters, after all."

He snorted back: "Which, without a huge promotion, would have flashed in the pan only to be replaced by the next cocktail fad." He eyed me. "You don't really think people care about quality cocktail ingredients, do you? They only care that quality cocktail ingredients make them feel sophisticated and to impress their friends, to get the girls like the dashing Boone Linsenbigler."

I sighed. "All about the sizzle, not the steak, aye? So what's the pitch this time? After all that has happened, I would think that my brand is overexposed. How can you build me up from here?"

He returned a lopsided grin. "We can't. We don't have to. Terry's award-winning documentary has made it patently clear that you are now what Conglomerated was only pretending you were."

"Oh, am I now?" I waved a hand at the bungalow and the surroundings. "Look, Prentis, I'm a blue water fly bum, and that's it, and that's all I ever want to be. Line up the young blondes in bikinis! Look around. I'm on permanent vacation."

He sipped his drink slowly, nodding, then cocked his head. "We both know that's not true, don't we?"

I became angry. "What is it you want with me, Prentis? What is it everybody wants of me? Haven't I endured enough?" I found myself standing and nose-to-nose with Hargreaves.

He didn't flinch, his icy eyes on mine. He whispered: "Apparently not."

I turned and kicked my lawn chair over the railing, breathing hard, saying nothing.

He cleared his throat. "Linsenbigler, if I might dispense a little advice, whether or not you come back to Conglomerated, that instead of resisting your lot in life, it might be better to embrace it and make it your own. What we offer you is a safe platform to do exactly that. Yes, we want to use your image and story to promote your cocktail products, but in a different way. Our hero Boone Linsenbigler is no longer just a swashbuckling cocktail napkin hero. He's a humanitarian, a real hero, a savior, a survivor. Our intent is to go heavily with the promotional dollars into charities in your name. Buying Boone Linsenbigler products not only make a person more suave and sophisticated, it makes them a better person like Boone. A dollar of every sale to a cause."

"And likely charging a buck and a half extra for the privilege. So the plan is to drag me all over the world shilling booze in the name of humanity?"

"That's not the plan."

I turned, glaring. "Then what is *the plan?*"

"You do whatever you like. Go fishing anywhere, stay in the best hotels...or not." He glanced at the bungalow behind me. "Or you can stay here. We'll pay for it all, within reason. We just want to use your story, your new brand to..."

"And Terry?"

"I'm not sure he wants to come back now. Not after the success of his documentary on you. And I don't think he's the right man for this sort of promotion."

"And my new boogle cocktail bitters?" I have of course withheld the actual name of the 'boogle' fruit to protect the recipe, but you can be sure the new bitters contain tamarind and cloves.

He cleared his throat, waving a pinky at the bungalow. "Is that where you make it, with that chemistry set in there? Yes, we acquired a sample from a friendly blogger, and it tests favorably in the demographic. We'll produce and market it. If you like, you can even pen a cocktail book, like one of those cocktail companions, and our publishing wing will make it happen."

I leaned against the railing, that flickering sunlight on the sea somehow like God winking at me.

Secretly, I winked back.

Heaving a great sigh of emotional burden, I said: "Write it up, Prentis. Send it to Bubby, and we'll see."

He left the bottle, with me at the railing quietly cursing my fate, Odysseus lamenting the burden of Poseidon's curse.

***

At dusk, I walked down the beach toward the thatched shanty that was Drifters Reef, the bottle of bourbon dangling from my hand. The strings of Christmas lights and colored light bulbs illuminating the dirty windows were always a welcome sight.

Some bar patrons were chattering on the veranda under lantern strings, and one of them, a woman with her shirt tied at the midriff, took leave of her companions and approached. The bottom half was in white cut-offs.

The woman was none other than the vivacious, swarthy Miranda, the dance instructor from the Queen Mary with whom I'd had a liaison. She was also the namesake that the ZLF used to lure me to the Jane Street Hotel to be kidnapped. So you can only imagine my reaction when she reached out to me by text to say hello, find out how I was after what I'd been through: *Egad, not again!* But I phoned her back and it was indeed she. It turned out I had given her my cell number after all. Miranda's itinerary brought her ship to port nearby, so I invited her to come for a visit *chez moi*.

It had been over a year since the coronation. Longer since Sophie, for whom my heart ache had turned to a bittersweet memory. Companionship, however briefly, was due.

Miranda swayed down the beach and finally stopped in front of me.

"So how did it go with Conglomerated?"

I grinned. "Like a charm."

"I see." She jerked a thumb at the bar, and considered me sidelong. "Brandi said you gave her bottom a squeeze."

I stepped closer, laughing to myself. "It was a pat to her bottom. Look, I had to sell it. If she were actually my twenty-something girlfriend, that's exactly what I would do. I'd much rather have squeezed your bottom."

"I thought you patted?"

"I did." I put my arm around her, turning her toward the bar. "Unlike Brandi's, your bottom I would have squeezed."

Someone on the bar veranda began to tune up a guitar.

She slid her arm around my waist, laughing. "Oh, I see, very flattering, and so suave. Speaking of squeezing, did you manage to squeeze everything you wanted out of Conglomerated?"

"I believe so."

Miranda pushed her long, coffee hair to the side, her golden eyes flashing. "So this whole con to get them down here, the hard-to-get act, this actually worked?"

"It was a simple matter of using Terry and Bubby to tease them into it. Like teasing up a striped marlin. I needed them to be absolutely convinced that I was a womanizing beach bum who needed to be dragged back kicking and screaming from his permanent vacation. People want desperately what they can't have."

The guitar on the veranda began to strum a samba.

If I had learned anything over the past two years, it was that there's a distinct advantage to encouraging manipulators to think you're something other than you are, less than you are. It sure helped me to con the King's Council.

And Trimble.

And Putin.

And now Prentis assumed I was some anguished, ill-fated boozer that he could manipulate with all this rot about submitting to my fate.

Submitting to my fate. That's what I almost did with a gun barrel under my chin in that stinking forest. Yet I didn't submit to fate when I chased those phony ZLF, and I didn't submit to my fate and die on that island, and I didn't submit to fate with those pirates, and I didn't submit to my fate to be Putin's or Trimble's shill as King of Zarenga Chi.

The only thing I submitted to was love. *C'est la vie.*

Boone Linsenbigler had become a 'man of action' in defiance of his perceived lack of aptitude. How had this happened? Because I learned that if I did not act, I was doomed to forever be the dupe of the manipulators.

Miranda smirked, shaking her head at my audacity. "Boone, you really want to be back with a giant corporation like that?"

We walked hip-to-hip across the sandy beach, the sun's ginger glow on the dark ocean. The cheerfully shabby saloon was close at hand, the tonic of laughter and tinkling ice on air.

A flute joined the guitar's samba.

"Miranda, it may sound jolly to drop anchor on a tropical island, but soon enough the tides change and you realize it might be time to pass through the reef while you can. I spent my time in isolation and reoriented myself to proceed uninhibited. So, yes, I want back in – on my terms. I decided back on Toad Caye that I wasn't going to let them turn me into a has-been."

"And the cocktail book idea…the charities…you got all that?"

"All my ideas to make my life useful and less phony, and I had Terry pitch it to them as though I had no hand in it. Predictably, Conglomerated lived up to their sneaky reputation and could not resist stealing his idea without rehiring him. Bubby told them I was not even going to discuss the possibility, and when pressed, he said the only shot might be if Prentis went in person, and so he 'leaked' my location. Everything fell into place."

She nodded at the bottle in my hand. "Is that bottle the Oscar for Best Performance by a Master Cocktailer you're holding?"

"Might as well be." I spun her, and put my arms

around her warm, silky waist, her tanned arms finding their way around my neck. What a tonic she was.

"But there's no finer reward for winning the Oscar than a kiss from a beautiful leading lady."

She batted her eyelashes: "I'll drink to that."

CℲℲ℧

BRIAN M. WIPRUD

"THE LINSENBIGLER
COCKTAIL COMPANION"

COMING CHRISTMAS 2018

BRIAN M. WIPRUD

ABOUT THE AUTHOR

Brian M. Wiprud's previous novels have earned starred reviews from Kirkus, Publisher's Weekly and Library Journal. Winner of the 2003 Lefty Award, he has been nominated for Barry, Shamus and Choice awards, and been an Independent Bookseller's and regional bestseller. His books are available variously in large print, audiobook and Russian and Japanese translations, and have been optioned for film. He has also been widely published in fly fishing magazines to include American Angler, Fly Fisherman, Fly Tyer, Massachusetts Wildlife and Saltwater Fly Fishing.

Previous Novels

11. Linsenbigler the Bear
10. Linsenbigler
9. The Clause
8. Ringer
7. Buy Back
6. Feelers

5. Tailed
4. Crooked
3. Sleep with the Fishes
2. Stuffed
1. Pipsqueak

Made in the USA
Middletown, DE
31 December 2020